CARIBBEAN HIT

An Eve Wade Mystery

Karen Henderson

ISBN: 1983774855
ISBN 13: 9781983774850
Library of Congress Control Number: 2018900899
CreateSpace Independent Publishing Platform
North Charleston, South Carolina

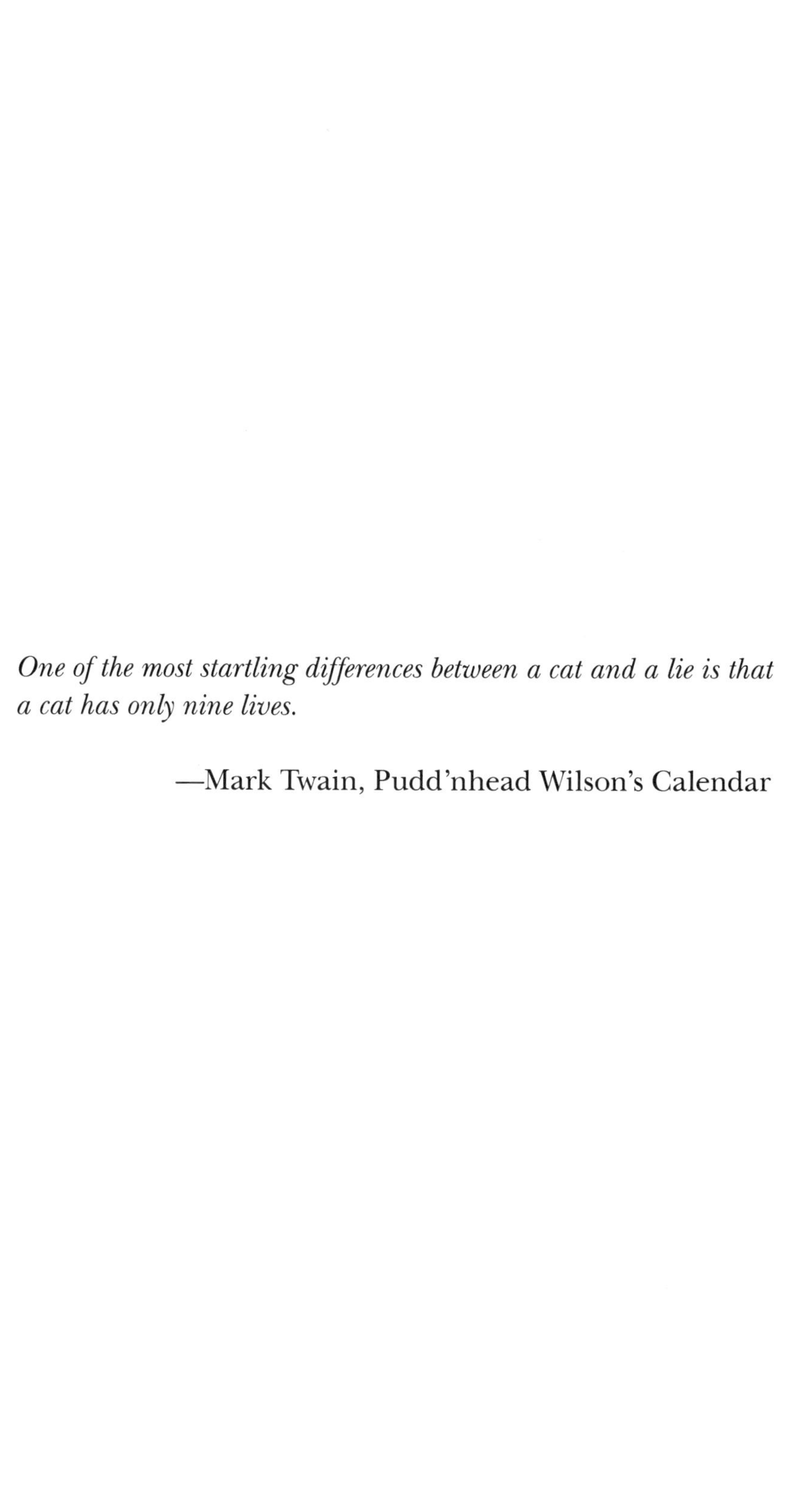

One of the most startling differences between a cat and a lie is that a cat has only nine lives.

—Mark Twain, Pudd'nhead Wilson's Calendar

PROLOGUE

A collision seemed inevitable. From the ship's bridge looming so many stories above, the odds of anyone spotting them in time were remote. Their small craft lay directly in its path dead in the water. The impact would surely squash them like a piece of flotsam in the vastness of the ocean. No one on board would feel the impact. No one would hear it. No one would come to their rescue if by some miracle they survived.

When Eve and her three companions first spotted the giant ship on the horizon, they cheered, believing help was at hand. Now all they could do was to cling to the sides of their nearly sunken boat, yelling and waving the remnants of her white T-shirt in the hope that someone would see them while the vessel still had time to veer from its present course. Otherwise, it would surely run them down, crushing them and their boat to smithereens.

Her vacation was supposed to be the trip of a lifetime—a barefoot cruise on a luxury yacht that had once belonged to a captain of industry. It was a trip Eve could never afford on her newspaper reporter's salary. The best part was that the week was free. All she had to do was to write a quick travel piece about what she thought was going to be the best getaway ever. Compared to her customarily gritty assignments for the *Cleveland Tribune*, the assignment would be a piece of cake for star investigative reporter Eve Wade.

Her newsroom colleagues were jealous of her good fortune. She was going to experience a terrific adventure, and she was getting out of the city during one of the coldest months of the year. In fact, her departure was made sweeter by the snow that had fallen the night before. It lay in graying piles on the highway as she took a taxi from the office to the airport. Now, she would give anything to be bundled up, tramping along a slush-covered sidewalk from the newsroom to a downtown assignment.

Eve wondered how things could have gone so horribly wrong in just a couple of days. She recalled with dismay her neighbor Irene's dire warnings about the dangers she would face if she took the cruise. Not a suspicious person herself, Eve had made fun of Irene's concerns and chalked them up to another of her oddities. Sometimes Eve could not help wondering if her eccentric friend who relied on tea leaves and tarot cards to plan her life could really see into the future. She hated the idea that Irene would be able to shake her turban-covered head and say knowingly, "I told you so." Of course, Eve would only hear it if she managed to get out of the current situation alive.

Her first inkling that the trip was jinxed should have been when the airline lost her luggage. The itinerary took them from island to island, allowing no time for her bag to catch up if it was found. But that was a minor glitch compared to what happened next.

A starker clue that the cruise was truly cursed was discovering two dead bodies aboard. She didn't remember seeing anything about dead people or a killer on board in the glossy brochure she had received from the cruise line prior to her departure. Had the graphic pictures been included, complete with blood spatter and brain matter on the wall, she undoubtedly would have stayed home. Even for a seasoned reporter used to covering homicides and other mayhem, excessive gore made her stomach churn. But it was too late for recriminations or hindsight.

She was adrift clinging to the side of a sinking boat that had been carried by the current into a main shipping lane. It was doubtful anyone on the *Sun Clipper* had seen them go down. They were already too far away when the boat began taking on water. By then, it was nearly dark, and they continued to drift away.

The behemoth that was about to crush them had first appeared as a dark shape in the distance. The throbbing engines initially brought joy to the stranded foursome. Rescue seemed to be at hand. However, as the ship got near enough that they could gauge its immense size, the realization dawned on them that no one on board would see them or hear their cries for help. They were but a speck on the infinite sea.

As if their plight were not dire enough, another danger had surfaced less than ten yards away. Eve was convinced she had glimpsed a dorsal fin slicing through the water. If the vessel somehow managed to miss them, they would be eaten by sharks before they could be rescued. As she mulled over this latest development, something large and slimy rubbed against her legs, and she did what came naturally under the circumstances. She screamed. Her distress brought hasty assurances from Charles, the Saint Vincent crewman who had accompanied them on this fool's errand, that the sharks and other sea creatures were not inclined to eat people. She was unconvinced, but hysterics would not chase them away.

In most of the hairy situations she had encountered during her sometimes dangerous career, she could usually choose the best option to pursue. In this case, there wasn't one, Eve realized. They could be dinner for one of the deadliest predators in the sea or be run over by one of its biggest ships. And if by some miracle neither of those unpleasant events occurred, they would surely drown. Land was nowhere in sight.

CHAPTER ONE

Burnout is about as common among newspaper reporters as the common cold is in the rest of the population. Two major symptoms include extreme tiredness that no normal amount of sleep can cure and an inability to get excited about assignments, even good ones.

Though only in her midthirties, Eve Wade was beginning to believe that she had been a reporter all her life. She had a hard time remembering ever doing anything else, including growing up. And for the past couple of years, she had been totally immersed in some of the most exciting but also the most depressing investigations of her career—pedophile priests who molested altar boys, con artists who scammed retirees out of their life savings, corrupt officials who pocketed taxpayers' money, gang members who terrorized communities, and an assortment of exceptionally brutal homicides. She frequently dealt with the walking-wounded, interviewing molested children and their grief-stricken mothers, hearing the accounts of elderly people who did not know how they would survive without their savings, and talking to the members of homicide victims' families. Her editor said she had a way with people who were suffering. "They open up to you," he would say.

The net result of her successes was that Eve was burned out. She was tired, and she needed a vacation.

It was Friday night after another eleven-hour day. Her boss, Wally O'Connell, a driven being himself, wasn't pleased when she told him she was taking a week off to go on a Caribbean cruise. It wasn't as if he hadn't known about her plans. She had been reminding him that she had vacation time coming for a month. It was in her contract.

"You can't go now. The mayor's about to be indicted," he whined, his voice sliding up the scale as it did when he wanted to make her feel particularly guilty. The mayor of one of the Cleveland suburbs the *Tribune* covered was about to be indicted for being too creative with his expense account. Eve had nailed him for charging the city thousands of dollars for business trips he never took.

"I've already done the investigative work. It's up to the prosecutor now. Anyone can write the indictment story," Eve argued. "I have the time saved. I've been invited. I'm going."

Wally gave her a dire look as she waved and headed for the door. If he was trying to make her feel guilty, he was failing miserably. She knew his guilt trips and bluster were just his way of keeping control of a newsroom teeming with reporters and their enormous egos.

"I need a break from all this death, destruction, and mayhem!" she yelled across the newsroom. At this time of night, she wasn't worried about disturbing anyone. The newsroom was nearly deserted of reporters, and the only people left were the poor souls who worked at the copydesk. "Maybe I'll even do a nice light travel story for you when I get back."

Wally managed a smile. "You wouldn't know how to write one. That's not your style. It would be too tame for you."

She made a face at him.

"Go on; have a good time. Get some rest," he said resignedly.

It took Eve about fifteen minutes to drive to her apartment, which was in an old brick building in what Clevelanders called an ethnic neighborhood and suburbanites referred to as a slum. She parked her car in the garage after wrestling with the automatic opener, which operated only when it wasn't cold or wet. Tonight it must have been cold. She had to get out of the car and raise the door manually, although the opener had no problem raising her neighbor's door across the street. So much for secure parking.

Inside her apartment, she was greeted by a flying feathered missile known as Keats, who landed on the top of her head. Keats was a spoiled and unusually affectionate parakeet. She lifted the bird from the part in her hair and set him on her shoulder.

While Keats flapped his wings to maintain his balance, she threw a load of clothes in the washer, pulled her old green Samsonite bag and a straw carry-on from the closet, and began searching through her drawers for shorts, T-shirts, and a turquoise bathing suit she had bought three years ago when she had gone to Florida. She hoped it still fit. Although the cruise was billed as casual, she packed a deep maroon-and-gold Indian dress of crinkle cotton that she had been saving for just such an occasion and threw in a pair of gold dress sandals. You never knew what might come up. To the growing pile, she added a pair of beaten-up leather buffaloes for the beach.

While she waited for her clothes to dry so she could finish packing, she deposited Keats on the top of his cage and ran across the street to Irene Chipek's house. She waited for several minutes and had almost decided her neighbor had either gone out or was asleep when Irene began turning the first of four locks on her kitchen door. Over the years since Eve had become friends with the older woman, she had adjusted to finding Irene in some rather strange costumes. But tonight Irene had outdone herself. She was clad in a tufted pink bathrobe and matching fluffy scuffs. A turban decorated with a huge bunny face and ears completed the ensemble, which would have been one of her more reserved outfits if it hadn't clashed so badly with the green goo that was hardening on her face.

"It's not contagious, is it?" Eve asked.

"Don't be smart. I was giving myself a facial. I didn't expect company at this time of night," Irene said, stepping aside to let Eve in.

"I just came to give you a key to the apartment so you can keep an eye on Keats for me. His seeds are on the kitchen counter. I've got some fruit and vegetables in the refrigerator for him."

"That bird hates me. He always bites me and leaves deposits on my head," Irene said.

"Wear a hat, but don't wear what you've got on. He's afraid of rabbits."

"I wish you weren't going," Irene said, ignoring her comment about the turban.

"Why, because of Keats?"

"No, I just have a bad feeling about this trip."

"Irene, you have bad feelings about every trip I take. You have bad feelings when I go to Dillard's to shop. Have you been reading tea leaves or cards or the entrails of chickens again?" Eve was convinced that some gypsy blood could probably be traced to Irene's Eastern European origins, which would account for her superstitious nature and the outlandish costumes she wore.

"Don't make fun of me, Eve. I just have bad vibes about this trip," Irene said, shaking her head. "I did do a reading this afternoon and—"

"I don't want to hear about it. I don't believe in that stuff, Irene. You know that. Are you sure you didn't get together with Wally? He's been plotting ways to get me to cancel all week."

Irene shook her head, and Eve saw that concern was reflected in the dark eyes that looked from behind the green goo. "I was right about Dillard's," Irene said. "That woman was abducted and murdered."

"That was from a parking lot three blocks away. If you had lived in Salem, you would have been burned as a witch," Eve said, but Irene wasn't listening.

"I saw death in the cards. Sunday will be a full moon. People go crazy when the moon is full," she said. "Don't go."

"Lighten up, Irene. If anything happens to me, I've willed Keats to you," Eve said, going to the door.

"Nothing better happen to you then, or I'll have the little beast stuffed and use him to decorate my hat," Irene replied, trying unsuccessfully to force a smile. Eve couldn't tell if her failure was due to lack of effort or to the green goo that had hardened her face into a permanent frown. Eve wasn't worried about Keats's welfare. Irene's love-hate relationship with the bird had served him well in the past. Last time Eve had been away, Irene had made him a pizza, which was one of his favorite foods as long as he could stand in the middle of it and take what he wanted.

"I'll send you and Keats a card from the tropics," Eve said.

"Better yet, bring back a nice man," Irene said.

Eve grinned and didn't respond as she pulled the door closed. Thrice married herself, Irene had two objectives where Eve was concerned. One was to fix her up with a husband—Eve was divorced—and the other was to protect her from the dangers Irene read in her cards.

Eve would never admit it to Irene, but her warning of impending peril had left Eve feeling a little deflated and uneasy. It seemed as if everyone was trying to talk her out of going on the cruise.

When she got home, the light on her answering machine was flickering. She depressed the play button, and steel-drum music throbbed in the background. Some of her enthusiasm returned when she found the message was from a woman at the *Sun Clipper* lines, who wanted her to know that a cruise-line representative would meet her plane in Saint Lucia. Mike Gardino, the pleasant-sounding man who had arranged the cruise for Eve by phone, would be driving her to the ship.

CHAPTER TWO

Mike Gardino wasn't sure whether it was the sticky air in the cabin or the fitful stirring of the woman who lay next to him in his narrow bunk that woke him. His cabin was about the size of a walk-in closet with a dresser, sink, and two narrow bunks stacked on top of each other. A combination shower and head occupied a space the size of a broom closet off the bedroom. The accommodations were not the kind of love nest he would have chosen, but the pretty red-haired nurse from Canada had not seemed to mind.

Months ago, he had come to the conclusion that being a cruise director on a sailing ship had its advantages. The booze was free, and on nearly every trip, he had a number of single women to choose from for companionship. Another advantage was that whatever happened in the seven- or fourteen-day cruise, the relationship would not lead to anything permanent. The last thing he wanted was a commitment. He had been on that route already, twenty years of marriage that ended two years ago when he had arrived home from work early one Friday afternoon. Marge and

Larry, his next-door neighbor and former best friend, were going at it in the king-size bed.

He had made a conscious effort not to think about the scene he had walked in on that day because it made him sick at heart each time he did. Dwelling on it, he was sure, would eventually drive him crazy. But sometimes when he'd had too much to drink, he saw again in painful detail how Marge's chestnut hair was spread out on the pillow. And he heard the sounds of their lovemaking reverberating through the quiet rooms.

He had packed his bags that night and left the house for good. Marge had tried to get him to stay. She had said that she wouldn't have had an affair if he had paid more attention to her. At the time, all he could think of was that his wife and his best friend had betrayed him. The man had even been wearing Mike's clothes. During the confrontation that afternoon, Larry had slipped on Mike's robe, which had been thrown over a chair next to the bed. Mike had remembered leaving it on a hook in the bathroom after he had showered that morning.

In the aftermath, when he relived the incident over and over in his mind, Mike had to admit that he was not blameless in the split. Marge was right. He had not spent that much time at home. There were nights when he had stayed in town when he should have been home. So perhaps it was his own sense of guilt and failure that made him leave as much as anything that was said or done that night.

He regretted leaving his sons, Kip and Andy. Kip was eighteen and Andy sixteen. They were still in high school, but despite his anger with Marge, he knew she was a good mother and that the boys would be better off left with her. The divorce had gone through quickly because he did not quarrel with her demands for the house and support for the boys, including help with college. Within six months, she had married the man who had taken his place at the table and whose name he still could not bring himself to say, although he was now stepfather to his sons.

Mike had liberal visitation rights, but he hated going to the house and seeing them together. He still thought of Marge as his wife. He guessed he always would. During the few times he had visited in the beginning, his mind was filled with dark, jealous thoughts. He imagined them making love in the bed he had shared with Marge for most of their years together. He could not seem to come to terms with the fact that she belonged to another man.

Now, as he lay in his cramped bunk and watched a beam of sunlight play across the polished wood of the cabin door, he tried not to begrudge Marge of her happiness. He only wished he was still part of it and that he could see more of his sons without feeling like his insides were being torn out of him each time he came to the house. The mental anguish had been intolerable, and six months after the divorce was final, he had escaped.

His escape, he thought with a hint of amusement, had not been a total success. He had distanced himself physically from Marge, but nothing short of a lobotomy would erase the painful memories.

"I can run, but I can't hide," he said out loud and then remembered Candy, who slept beside him. He watched the sunlight discover the blond highlights in her reddish hair. She was quite beautiful, a woman he hardly knew and would certainly never know long enough to love as he had Marge.

It was an advertisement in the *New York Times* for a cruise director for the *Sun Clipper* line that had caught his eye and had eventually landed him where he was. He was obviously overqualified and had a problem convincing the owner of the small Miami-based line, Albert Sinclair, that he would be able to live on a salary that was less than six figures and only a fraction of what he had earned in the high-pressure world of advertising within six months of leaving Columbia. In the end, Sinclair had agreed to take a chance on him because he was the most qualified applicant, and the struggling cruise line needed his promotional expertise.

Because the line's advertising budget was limited, he had convinced Sinclair that the best publicity they could get would be from articles written by reporters and travel writers who were given free cruises. Sinclair had balked at the plan at first because he hated to have nonpaying passengers taking up space on his ships, but Mike pointed out that most cruises were not selling out anyway, and this was a way to generate paying customers without spending much for advertising. It had taken Mike little time on the job to discover that free travel in return for positive press was one of the most common ways the travel industry sold itself. A good feature story in a travel section of a large newspaper was worth thousands of dollars of paid advertising in the same paper.

After Sinclair reluctantly agreed, Mike set about contacting writers and reporters all over the country. He tried to select those who reached a broader audience with their writing, and he targeted the more heavily populated areas of the East Coast and the Midwest, surmising that they were closer to the Caribbean, thus making air fares lower, and the winter weather in these states was usually pretty harsh. Few of the writers he contacted passed up the offer of a free Caribbean cruise.

Mike learned that most newspapers lacked policies or writers scruples that prevented them from accepting freebies. And even the newspapers and magazines that did have policies against their own writers accepting free trips quite illogically accepted articles written by freelance writers who accepted them. Mike also found, although there was never a written agreement that the articles would be positive, few writers risked becoming too critical for fear of missing out on future invitations. Newspaper reporters were notoriously underpaid and coveted those free trips, not to mention the free booze and meals that were included.

If Sinclair had been skeptical about the cost versus what he would get in exposure, he soon changed his mind when positive stories about *Sun Clipper* cruises began showing up in major newspapers and magazines across the country, and the phone lines in the tiny office began lighting up with calls from travel agents and private individuals wanting to book tours. He had to hire extra office staff to handle the inquiries and orders that flooded in. Mike also spiced up the messages on the office answering machine and call waiting, playing island steel-drum music and getting an actor with an island accent to read promos for the line.

With sales soaring, after a few months, Sinclair added another tall ship to the line, bringing the size of his fleet to four. Business was good, and Sinclair showed his gratitude by giving Mike a raise and his own cabin on working cruises. Part of Mike's job was to go on the cruises and to make sure the writers had a memorable time. Good food, free-flowing booze, and the sunny Caribbean weather usually helped guarantee positive articles. Emphasizing the good points of the cruise and minimizing the negative ones, including the tiny cabins typical of sailing vessels, was all part of his job.

Most of the time, Mike enjoyed his work, although he found he was starting to put on weight and was drinking too much. At least the booze and female companionship kept his mind off what he referred to as his recent less-than-illustrious past.

Sometimes Mike suffered a few pangs of remorse when one of his romances ended and he had to tell the woman he had no plans to continue the relationship when she went home—usually to the States, Europe, or Canada. Mike soothed his conscience by telling himself her pain would not last long because vacation romances were like that. They usually faded by the time the pictures were printed out. After a couple of phone calls and a few letters, the relationship ended with neither party being hurt too badly. In Mike's still-wounded state, this was the best he could do.

Now Mike shifted in the bunk, trying to get a look at the clock next to the bed without disturbing Candy. He could tell by the light flooding the cabin through the single porthole next to the top bunk that it was well into the morning. He could also tell by the absence of the throbbing of the diesel engines that they had already made port, and he should be on deck.

Contrary to popular belief, the sailing ships used by the cruise line rarely made way under sail. It was impossible to keep a schedule if you depended on the wind. The sails were often raised during the day but more for show than anything else. Passengers who fancied themselves sailors were encouraged to heave on the lines while relatives or friends snapped pictures and selfies for the album. The billowing white sails provided memorable photo opportunities. On calm days, the captain would put down the johnboat and allow the passengers to take turns shooting the ship from some distance away. The pictures would later be passed around the office and shown to friends and relatives who became potential customers. Nobody seemed to mind that the tall sailing ships, most formerly the pleasure yachts of captains of industry, really didn't sail anymore even when the sails were hoisted.

Mike found the whole thing rather amusing. He got a perverse pleasure out of watching middle-aged, overweight passengers hauling on the lines or arguing over whose turn it was to take the wheel for a few minutes. All in all, it was an easier life than he had led before, and it was not without its benefits. Money wasn't everything, he thought as he edged his way out of the bunk to avoid waking Candy.

It was time to get to work. He had eight writers this trip, and he needed to keep them interested and happy. Happy writers wrote positive stories. He had already missed the first contingent at breakfast. The passengers ate in two shifts because the dining room was too small to accommodate everyone at one sitting, and he was in danger of missing the second sitting if he didn't get moving. Fortunately, most of the writers liked to party and had signed up for the late shift. If he hurried, he still had time to sit down with them in the dining room. He was not concerned about missing breakfast. His aching head and upset stomach told him he had drunk too much the night before, and the last thing he wanted was food.

Trying to be as quiet as possible, he stepped into the bathroom and rinsed off under the trickle of lukewarm water that ran from the shower head. He had learned to go lightly on the shampoo and soap because they were hard to rinse off given the low water pressure on the ship. A few minutes later, he stepped from the bathroom and pulled on shorts and a *Sun Clipper* T-shirt. His bare feet completed his working uniform. It beat the starched shirt, power tie, and polished toe-pinching wingtips he had worn those many years when he toiled on Madison Ave.

Mike saw that Candy had sprawled across the bed, taking up the space he had just left. She was still asleep. He closed the door quietly behind him and headed up the corridor to work.

CHAPTER THREE

The sun was a golden orb in the eastern sky. Its reflection on the waves turned the sea into a shimmering carpet of blue. It was a glorious morning in the tropics with a gentle breeze stirring and hardly a cloud in the sky. Eve sipped her second glass of orange juice and enjoyed the view from the upper deck. She had passed up the complimentary bloody marys being served at a beverage counter on deck and the breakfast of corn flakes, scrambled eggs, bacon, and toast being served in the dining room below. It was too early to drink, she thought, but she could see by the line of passengers waiting at the bar that many did not share her opinion. Of course, a lot of people just couldn't pass up anything that was included in the travel package.

Booze and heavy food in the morning held no appeal for her. Some fresh fruit would have been nice, but none had been available at last night's or this morning's meals. Although the ship was cruising among islands known for their exotic spices and fruits, she was disappointed to find that the food was typically American; she hesitated to call it cuisine, a term she usually saved for dining that was a cut above average. So far, the food aboard the *Sun Clipper* did not meet this criterion, and she suspected from the canned fruits and frozen vegetables at supper that everything had probably been purchased in the States.

In the distance, she could see the island of Bequia, their first stop since she had joined the ship the night before in Saint Lucia. The johnboat and a small launch were already being lowered to ferry the passengers to the tiny town nestled behind the horseshoe-shaped harbor or to the sandy white beach that gleamed in the sunlight on the portside of the ship. Some of the passengers were assembling on the deck below in hopes of being among the first to go ashore. The islanders who worked as deckhands for the cruise line would operate the boats most of the day, ferrying passengers between the ship and shore. The boats would bring many of the passengers back for lunch and then return them to shore in the afternoon. The final trip back to the ship was to be at 4:30 p.m. because the ship would sail soon after. Those were the captain's instructions given during a morning briefing and posted in a notice written in bold print on the dining-room bulletin board for those who had overslept and missed the briefing.

This was Eve's first full day on board, and she was looking forward to going ashore. The cruise was already in its second week when she had joined it in Saint Lucia. A week was all the vacation time she could get, and she had had to fight to get that much. But she had been more interested in the second leg of the trip than the first, anyway, because it visited the less-inhabited islands. The first leg hit the tourist and shopping islands from Puerto Rico south.

Eve had always loved to travel from the time she was a little girl, and the family spent a week each summer at a cottage on Georgian Bay in Canada. Travel offered a means of escape, whether it was from her job or a family crisis. Sometimes she wished she had been born rich so she could spend her life wandering around the world visiting exotic places and meeting exciting people instead of wading through the filth of the city to write about the human devastation she saw each day.

Eve was born Evita Wade thirty-five years ago, and when she was still in grade school, she decided that it was bad enough to live in Cleveland, Ohio, the center of the industrial "rust belt," without having to be saddled with a name like Evita. She wasn't even Spanish or Latino, for heaven's sake. Eve understood her mother's theatrical flair, but for the life of her, Eve could not understand why a woman who professed to love her had named her for a prostitute who later became the wife of an Argentine dictator. Her mother was of English and Scandinavian descent, and her father was Manx, though most kids Eve grew up with didn't know what Manx was. Even most adults who had heard of the Isle of Man, nestled in the Irish Sea between England and Ireland, only knew that it was famous for Manx cats. "Aren't those the ones that are born looking like their tails got chopped off in the screen door?" she was frequently asked. Little Evita could not change her odd place of paternal ancestry. But when she was sixteen, she obtained her parents' permission to change her name legally to Eve.

Eve inherited her blond-haired, blue-eyed Scandinavian looks from her mother's side of the family, but she inherited her writing ability from her father's. Eve's Manx ancestors were an eccentric mix of writers, scholars, and farmers, the latter profession often chosen in collaboration with the first two because it was what put food on the table. It was Eve's Manx grandmother who taught her a love of books and writing by spending hours reading to her when she was a child. She had decided at a tender age, while nudging her grandmother in the ribs to keep her from nodding off while reading *King Arthur* or some other equally fascinating tale from one of the *Oz* books that she too would be a writer someday.

After graduating from high school and while still a teenager, Eve made her way overseas, where she began a writing career, freelancing for magazines and eventually landing a job with a newspaper in the Middle East. After a few years of living a vagabond life abroad and with her father in failing health, she had returned to Cleveland and gone to work for the local newspaper. Cleveland was a tough place to grow up, but it was an investigative reporter's dream. Public corruption was rampant in government, and Eve liked nothing better than to rout it out. That was probably why she still lived there.

She loved to travel, but she was not a travel writer. What she considered light, bright, and trite writing had never appealed to her. Her expertise lay in hard news and investigative reporting. As she leaned against the railing soaking up the rays of the morning sun so unlike the gray gloom she had left behind when she boarded her plane in Cleveland, she was already thinking of a poetic beginning for the freelance piece she would write when she got back. It wasn't only that her first glimpse of Bequia had moved her to want to write, but on the practical side, a travel piece would allow her to write off some of the expenses, which were going to be higher than she had anticipated.

The cruise was free, but she had paid for her airfare and then been forced to buy new clothes from the ship's store because the airline had lost her luggage. A seasoned traveler and well aware of the airlines' proclivity to spoil vacations by losing luggage, she had packed her camera, bathing suit, a change of underwear, shorts, and a T-shirt in a carry-on bag. That would not be enough to get her through a week, and she was glad the ship had a store that usually opened in the dining room every afternoon.

Mike, the cruise director who undoubtedly believed happy reporters would write positive stories, had gotten the purser to open the store especially for her the night before and had given her a "lost luggage" clothing discount on shorts and shirts. Now, she mused, she looked like a walking advertisement for the cruise line. She would survive without the dress and sandals she had packed. And if anyone got tired of seeing her either barefoot or in tennis shoes, that was too bad. After all, the week of island-hopping was billed as a barefoot cruise.

Before they left the airport, Mike had telephoned the ship to get their itinerary so the airline would know where the *Sun Clipper* might be docked if the bag were found. But it was unlikely, even if the airline found her errant bag, that it would catch up with the ship, which sailed to a different island each night—many too small to have airports. In any case, the itinerary often changed with the weather.

Word had spread among the fifty-six passengers about her lost luggage before she arrived on board. As she walked up the gangway, several had been waiting to welcome her and to offer to loan her clothing. Eve had been a little embarrassed by the unexpected attention and had politely declined the offers.

A gaudily dressed middle-aged woman, who wore too much makeup and looked like she had spent the day having her bleached hair coiffed and her nails painted, was very insistent. "My name's Florence, but just call me Flo. Everybody does," she said, patting Eve on the arm. "I've got more clothes than I'll ever be able to wear even if I stay another month. Come on down to the cabin, and pick out whatever you need." Her speech was slurred, and Eve surmised, though it was just past nine o'clock, that Flo had indulged in too many of the island rum drinks.

Her husband, a short, dark-haired man who extended his hand and introduced himself as Tony, urged her to accept his wife's offer. "My wife has cleaned out every store from Puerto Rico south. I've had to buy four new suitcases, and the trip is only half over. I don't know how we'll ever get this stuff back to Chicago or what we'll do with it when we get there. If you take some clothes, maybe I can at least have a place to sleep." He laughed and squeezed Eve's arm until she gently dislodged it from his grasp. Both meant well, but neither had taken into consideration that Flo was a size sixteen and Eve a petite size six.

"If they don't find my bag, maybe I'll take you up on your offer," Eve said. It seemed the only tactful way to get rid of them. As she made her escape behind a deckhand who had been assigned to show her to her cabin, she wondered why Tony and Flo spoke with Bronx accents if they were from Chicago. Maybe they had moved there from New York, she thought and scolded herself for immediately questioning the veracity of people she had just met. It had become a hazard of her profession to question everything and everyone. It was a trait she hated in herself. Before leaving home, she had promised herself to leave her investigative reporter's instincts behind and to simply enjoy the trip. That was easier said than done, but she was determined not to let anything, including her lost clothing, ruin the trip. She usually packed too much, anyway. Now she would find out just how little she could get by with.

She had not slept well the first night, although she was exhausted by the time she had reached the ship. The flight from Cleveland to Saint Lucia, with a change of planes in Miami, had taken most of the day because of an unexplained delay in Miami and a second delay in Saint Lucia that occurred while airline officials searched for her bag. When they finally acknowledged what Eve already knew, that it was lost, another delay occurred while they searched for the right forms for her to fill out. The forms contained a description of the bag and its contents so they could begin to trace its whereabouts. All this activity had taken nearly an hour when it should have taken less than ten minutes. The attendants made phone calls to Miami and then held lengthy discussions among themselves about what should be done and which form should be used, as if luggage weren't lost every day. Eve's mind was still working on Cleveland time, but she began telling herself to adjust to island time, which she compared to pushing the pause button on the VCR.

She had then boarded a van that bounced over a deeply rutted road from the airport to the port of Castries on the other side of the island where the ship was docked. The trip across the island was made in the dark, and she regretted not being able to see much besides the ruts in the road outlined in the headlights.

Mike had met her and another writer named Jerry Addison and ridden back with them in the van. The other reporters had begun the cruise the week before and were already on board. Addison, who wrote for a Toronto travel magazine Eve had never heard of, was miffed with the delay at the airport. His luggage had arrived, and he apparently saw no reason to spend a lot of time waiting to see what had happened to hers. Addison was a tall, sandy-haired man with startling blue eyes and a good build. Eve guessed him to be in his late thirties or early forties. She would have found him quite attractive if he had not been such a prick. Instead, she found herself taking an immediate dislike to him.

Addison had said very little on the trip across the island, leaving it up to Mike to carry on the conversation. Eve usually had a reporter's low opinion of ingratiating public-relations types, but she liked Mike in spite of her bias. He was black-haired, brown-eyed, and affable, and his concern over her lost luggage appeared to be sincere.

Now, while Eve sipped her juice and tilted her face to better catch the warmth of the morning sun, she saw Mike appear at the top of the stairs. He glanced around and smiled in her direction before heading to the juice table and pouring himself a large glass. Though he appeared to be freshly showered and shaved, he looked a little spent. During the previous evening, at least what was left of it when she arrived, he had been accompanied by an attractive red-haired woman whom Eve suspected was probably the reason he looked so tired this morning.

It also had taken Eve only a short time to decide that Mike probably had a drinking problem. The ship, which had been waiting to leave port, had gotten underway almost as soon as they arrived. The bar was already open and the noise level rising. After introducing Eve to the purser and the treasures of the ship's store, Mike had found his way to the bar and appeared to be trying to match everyone on board drink for drink. He was obviously paying the price this morning with a considerable hangover.

Eve walked to the portside of the ship to get a better view of the tiny island that lay in the distance. Mountains covered with dense green foliage rose steeply behind the town that ringed the sandy white beach. She could see a row of small shops painted in pastel colors along a road that followed the contour of the harbor. From a distance, Bequia appeared to be a beautiful place, and Eve could not wait to go ashore to explore it.

She was about to make her way to the deck below where a ladder was being lowered to the boats when Mike appeared at her side.

"Beautiful morning," he said.

"Yes," Eve replied.

"How'd you sleep?"

"Not too well, but it usually takes me a night to adjust to a new bed," she said. "The engines seem to be rather loud. I guess I expected a sailing ship to sail quietly."

She could see Mike's handsome public-relations face adjusting. He was undoubtedly wondering whether the loss of her luggage and a sleepless first night would mean that a half million Ohio readers would be told not to take a *Sun Clipper* cruise. His concern was so obvious it almost made her laugh.

"We have to have the right winds to sail, and most of the time, we couldn't keep to a schedule if we relied on the winds to propel the ship," he said. "We did sail more often during the first week because we had better winds." Eve was not inclined to try to disprove this statement, though she rather doubted, based on her first night's experience, that much sailing went on during any cruise.

Switching to a more positive subject, Mike said, "You're going to love Bequia. It's one of the most beautiful islands we visit."

It was Sunday, perhaps one of the loveliest Sundays Eve could remember. She thought about Irene and her dire warnings and the gray snow that had lain like so much dirty laundry along the highways on the way to Cleveland Hopkins Airport the day before.

"Eat your heart out, Irene," she said.

"Did you say something?" Mike asked. Eve had forgotten about him.

"I was just talking to my neighbor."

She left Mike standing at the railing, looking confused as she went below to catch the boat to Bequia.

CHAPTER FOUR

The Caribbean breezes and the boat traffic in the harbor caused the launch to pitch and rock as it made the fifteen-minute crossing from the *Sun Clipper* to the dock. Eve was seated near the stern, and spray dampened her face as the boat struck the waves. She found it refreshing, but Flo, who once again looked like she had spent hours at the hairdresser, was complaining that the wind and spray were ruining her do.

It was an odd group. There was Flo, slathered with oil over her heavy makeup and trying to hold her hair in place with her hand. Next to her were the Overtons, freelance writers from a small town in Massachusetts, who were desperately hanging onto huge straw hats they wore to shade their faces from the Caribbean sun. The Overtons appeared to be in their thirties but acted much older, Eve thought. They had already been on the cruise for a week before Eve joined it, yet both had snow-white skin, and Oliver Overton had an unnatural pallor to his complexion.

During their first conversation, which had taken place just before boarding the launch, Cecilia Overton had told Eve she was afraid of getting skin cancer and hated the sun. She said her husband had a skin condition and was allergic to the sun, which left Eve wondering why they had come to the Caribbean. Visiting a mushroom farm in Manitoba might have made for a better Overton vacation, Eve thought, although she wasn't sure if Manitoba had mushroom farms. Both Overtons also wore long-sleeved shirts, pants, and sunglasses.

In contrast to the time it must have taken Flo and Tony Mason and the Overtons to get ready, Eve figured it had taken only minutes for her to become a walking billboard for the cruise line in her *Sun Clipper* shirt and shorts. One thing about losing your luggage was that it took away any prolonged decision-making about selecting the right outfit to wear. Flo was wearing a red top and shorts splotched with pictures of green parrots and large island flowers. Her red lipstick, fingernail and toenail polish, and a beaded necklace matched the red in the background of her outfit. Eve wondered how early Flo had gotten up to have time to do her hair, makeup, and nails so that everything matched. She was obviously showing off some of her island clothing purchases. They were not even the kind of thing Flo would wear in Chicago.

Tony sat quietly next to Flo on the narrow bench. Somewhat hidden from Eve's view by his wife's bulk, he seemed thinner than he had the night before. His dark eyes, shaded by sunglasses, darted from one passenger to another. In contrast to his wife's showy outfit, Tony was conservatively dressed. Gone were the canary-yellow shorts and Hawaiian print shirt of the night before. He wore a white cotton shirt open at the neck and a pair of khaki walking shorts. He was dark skinned and heavily tanned.

Jerry Addison sat in the bow of the launch, and he too appeared to be watching the people in the boat instead of the scenery. He had merely nodded to Eve when he saw her in the morning, and Eve surmised he was still angry that her lost luggage had held him up the night before. What an unfriendly guy, she thought. How out of character for a travel writer. Most were outgoing people, some a little odd like the Overtons, but they were definitely outgoing.

Two young honeymooners, completely absorbed in one another, sat next to Addison. They also were not watching the scenery. The mountains loomed larger, forming a green backdrop to the tiny town, as the boat neared the shore. The sandy beaches, which Eve had first seen from the deck, appeared even whiter now, and the water was so clear that when she looked over the side of the boat, she glimpsed colorful fish swimming among the reefs. She had chosen to go to town to look around before catching the launch to the beach.

Mike and several passengers who had been here before had suggested she stop by Melinda's, a shop famous in the islands for beautiful hand-painted clothing. Melinda, it was said, was a transplanted American who had been lured to the islands by a seafaring man. The relationship had not worked out, but she had remained on the island, turning her considerable talents into a profitable business. Her hand-painted birds and tropical flowers were famous, and everyone who went to Bequia shopped at her store. Eve was not much of a purchaser of island T-shirts and souvenirs, but the simple fact was that she needed clothes.

The two crewmen steadied the launch as the passengers climbed onto the dock. Because she sat in the stern, Eve was one of the last out. With the exception of Jerry Addison and herself, the other passengers had already been on the ship for a week and had formed friendships. Now they headed out in small groups. Eve had no interest in pairing up with Jerry. The feelings appeared to be mutual because Jerry had disappeared by the time Eve reached the dock. Eve saw Flo start to hang back to wait for her, but she was grateful when Tony took his wife by the arm and hustled her toward town. Eve did not mind being alone; in fact, she enjoyed traveling alone so she did not have to worry about having her own plans conflict with those of a traveling companion.

When she reached the main street, she turned right, heading in the direction of Melinda's shop. As she passed the first row of stores, shopkeepers called to her and tried to interest her in their brightly painted T-shirts. Parrots seemed to be the T-shirt design of choice for Bequia tourists, judging by what hung in the shop windows. Eve wandered in and out of several shops on her way up the street. It was a little after ten in the morning, and some of the shopkeepers were just opening for business, the openings apparently timed to the arrival of the *Sun Clipper*'s tourists and an even larger group descending from a large cruise ship that had anchored in the harbor some distance from the *Clipper.* As Eve walked up the street, she could see the tenders from the larger ship beginning to shuttle back and forth. The tiny island was about to become crowded. Shopkeepers alerted to the arrival of the two ships were moving into high gear, scurrying about and preparing their shops for the invasion of tourists with cash and credit cards.

Eve passed a couple of small bars and restaurants that were just opening for business. A small boy, who Eve judged to be about eight, was sweeping the tile patio in front of one of them. He smiled and beckoned to Eve to come in.

"It's too early to drink," Eve said.

"We have Coca Cola," he said, apparently raised in the belief that that was the nonalcoholic beverage preferred by most Americans. Eve was thirsty. She had not yet adjusted to the heat, which she judged to be already in the middle eighties. She hesitated for a moment and then turned and caught a glimpse of the building's dark interior. It looked cool, and the thought of something cold to drink lured her inside. She was standing at the bar, trying to convince the bartender that she did not want rum in her Coca Cola, that being the only nonalcoholic beverage he offered, when movement in the rear of the darkened room caught her eye.

She did a quick double-take. Seated in a dark corner was Jerry Addison deep in conversation with a man Eve had not seen before.

As Eve stared, Addison, who was sitting with his back to the wall, looked in her direction. When their eyes met, Eve could feel his hostility. Obviously he had not expected to see anyone from the ship, least of all the person who had made him late for his cruise. Eve's curiosity was certainly aroused, and she was tempted to wander over to say something to Jerry just to get a look at the man he was with. But the menacing look he shot in her direction told her that was not a good idea.

Her mind was working again. Who was Addison, really? She had never heard of the travel magazine he worked for, and he did not act like a reporter or writer because he was just too unfriendly. You could not get stories if you never made friends. Besides, Eve had decided that Addison did not have a Canadian accent. Of course, it was sometimes hard to detect some Canadian accents, but most people who came from the Toronto area where Addison said he was from said things like "aboot" for "about." Addison had not talked a lot during their van trip across Saint Lucia, but he had talked enough for Eve to notice the accent was wrong. If she were a gambling woman, Eve would have bet that Addison was from the United States and, like herself, probably from the Midwest.

And who was this other man, and where had he come from? Although Eve had been on the ship for only a day, she was pretty sure she had seen all the passengers. It was a small ship with only fifty-six passengers, and most had been at breakfast, on deck or in the bar the night before. It was possible he was someone who had stayed in his cabin, but how had he gotten to shore in the morning without Eve seeing him? She had come over in the first launch, and he was not on it. She was sure of that. Perhaps that was why Addison was in such a hurry to get on shore when they arrived and why he had disappeared so quickly. Eve guessed it was because he had a prearranged appointment to keep in Bequia, of all places.

Eve thought it unlikely that the unfriendly Jerry Addison just happened to run into someone he knew in a place as out of the way as this. The man with Addison also looked American. He was dark haired and tall like Addison, and he wore tourist garb, T-shirt, white tennis shorts, and Reeboks. But despite his casual dress, Eve guessed he was not a tourist, or at least had not been one for long, because his arms and legs appeared quite white even in the darkened room. Eve was unable to get a good look at his face because his back was to her, and to her disappointment, he did not turn around. She smiled at Addison, who continued to glare at her. Conversation at the table had been suspended.

Eve decided against approaching the two. She raised her Coke as if to toast Addison, sipped it, and then turned to leave. Addison continued to scowl at her but raised his hand in weak acknowledgment of her friendly gesture. She walked away feeling uneasy and wondering what Addison was up to. Whatever it was, Eve reminded herself, it was none of her business. Under her breath, she began the familiar lecture to herself, "Stop being a snoopy reporter. Enjoy the trip." The little boy, who was still sweeping the patio, gave her an odd look as she passed him, Coke in hand, still muttering to herself.

It was hard to change, and unfounded suppositions filled her mind as she walked. Maybe Addison was a drug dealer meeting his island connection. Maybe they were planning to use the *Clipper* to smuggle drugs into the States. She doubted that almost as much as she doubted that he was a writer or Canadian.

It became easier to put Jerry Addison and his mystery acquaintance out of her mind once she was inside Melinda's shop. Melinda's hand-painted flowers and birds were works of art. Eve chose a T-shirt with a picture of a mythical Doctor Bird painted on it. It was made of light-weight cotton that she could hand-wash and dry in the cabin overnight. Several other *Sun Clipper* passengers, including Flo, were already in the shop. Flo had stacked several items on the counter by the time Eve went to pay for her T-shirt.

"Which do you like?" she asked, holding up two T-shirts with different paintings of birds.

"I like them both," Eve said.

"Then I'll take them both." Flo laughed and tossed them onto a growing pile of clothing on the counter. "Christmas gifts for the grandkids," she said.

Somehow Eve doubted this unless her grandchildren came in large sizes.

"They'll love them," Eve said. "Where's Tony?"

At the mention of his name, Flo appeared nervous. "He's tired of shopping," she said. "He went back to the ship."

Eve could understand how easy it would be to tire of both Flo and shopping. She would not have blamed him if he were in a bar somewhere getting drunk. She paid for her purchase and said good-bye to Flo, who seemed to have no plans to leave as long as there were any clothes left on the racks. Eve headed further up the street looking at the picturesque stucco homes painted in pastel colors. Wash hung on balconies and on lines in the small patios, where brightly colored tropical flowers bloomed. After a few minutes of walking, she turned back toward the harbor. She had worn her bathing suit under her clothes and had stuffed a towel in the large straw bag she carried. She planned to take the launch to the beach when she was finished shopping.

Unfortunately, when the airline lost her luggage, it had also lost her mask and snorkeling fins. If there was one thing that Eve found completely relaxing, it was snorkeling on a Caribbean reef. She had learned to snorkel during a cruise several years earlier. Her first trip out, she had used rented equipment and been given a leaky rubber mask that turned her face black. Despite looking as if she cleaned chimneys for a living and choking on the salt water that seeped into the mask, she had found looking at the fish and other sea creatures one of the most fascinating things she had ever done. Back home, she had bought her own mask and fins and now carried them with her on trips.

Mike had promised to loan her his mask and to find her a pair of fins by the time she got to the beach. He had assured her the snorkeling was good at either end of the sandy area where rocks jutted into the sea. During the morning briefing, the captain had said the crew would bring lunch for those who did not want to return to the ship. That had sounded like a wonderful idea, and Eve had put in her order.

Now, as she began looking forward to an afternoon of snorkeling and sunning herself, she quickened her pace. She slowed down when she passed the bar where she had seen Addison and the stranger earlier, but after lingering long enough for her eyes to adjust to the darkened interior, she could see that they were no longer inside.

She continued up the street and probably would not have noticed anything at all if she had not heard a taxi beep its horn behind her. As she turned to look back, she found herself looking directly into an alley that ran uphill toward the base of the mountain. About a block up the hill, she caught sight of Jerry Addison talking to someone who stood in the shadows of a building. Eve suspected it was probably the same man she had seen with Addison in the bar. It appeared that he and Addison were arguing because Addison was shaking his finger at him.

It was not until the man in the shadows stepped into the alley that she realized it was someone she did know. She had seen the khaki shorts and tan legs that morning. The man Addison was giving a hard time was none other than Tony Mason. And it appeared, when Eve crossed the street to the other side of the alley, that Tony was also very angry. Eve could not hear what was being said, but she could hear a whine in Tony's raised voice and see him gesturing at Addison with his arms.

Not wanting to be spotted snooping, she reluctantly continued up the street toward the harbor. Who was Jerry Addison? she wondered for the second time that day. And how did he already seem to know so many people intimately enough to get into deep conversations and even arguments with them? She was struck by yet-another thought, that either Flo had lied when she said her husband was going back to the ship or there were things Tony did not tell his wife. She also remembered Addison's glances at Tony while they were in the launch. They apparently knew each other and had acted as if they were strangers. How odd.

Eve shifted her straw bag to her other hand and, exhibiting an astonishing degree of self-discipline, forced herself to suppress her natural curiosity. Once more, she reminded herself that her only goal was to have a good time and to write a good travel story when she got back. As she continued walking to the pier, she pushed thoughts of Addison, the stranger, and the Masons out of her mind. She concentrated on the travel story she would write and her first impressions of Bequia. If she wrote a good story, she mused, she might even be invited back next year.

CHAPTER FIVE

Some of the *Sun Clipper* passengers were already at the beach when Eve arrived and spread her towel in the shade of a scrubby tree. She saw Mike a little distance away surrounded by a group of women that included the redhead. Eve had not met any of them yet, but she had found out from the Overtons that they were Canadian nurses. Shortly after she had settled herself on the beach and opened a dog-eared novel by Sara Paretsky that she had taken from the ship's library of paperbacks, Mike joined her.

"Here's the mask," he said, handing her what appeared to be a better snorkeling mask than the one in her missing luggage. "Try it on and see if it fits," he said. After adjusting the strap and pulling it on, Eve was pleased to find that it did. "I had more trouble getting a pair of flippers in your size. Mine are a size eleven, and you wouldn't be able to keep them on your feet. One of the crew had a pair with an adjustable strap," Mike said, producing a well-worn pair from the beach bag he was carrying.

Eve assured him they would probably be fine. Producing a pair of white tube socks from the bag, he suggested she wear them under the flippers to protect her from the coral and to take up some of the extra width because the flippers were in a man's size. Eve thanked him, and Mike nodded and walked back to his female companions.

Laying her book aside, Eve decided to check out the snorkeling near the end of the beach that was farthest away from town. The water was warm and clear, and she was immediately treated to a mesmerizing underwater world. A green-and-red parrot fish swam in and out of crevices in the rock formations that jutted out from the beach. A school of dark-blue and yellow fish followed her, seeming to be as curious about her as she was about them.

Her fascination with the palette of color she found in the coral reef and among the fish made her lose all track of time. Sometimes she swam and sometimes she hung suspended in the water, barely moving her feet to keep afloat while she watched what was happening below her. A few other snorkelers invaded her area from time to time, but after a while she was more or less alone. She was a strong swimmer, having been on her high-school swim team, but she stayed within sight of the beach, knowing it was better to be cautious. Mike had also made a point of warning her not to go beyond the promontory jutting out beyond the reef because of the strong currents.

An hour or more had passed when Eve became aware of someone swimming close to her in the water. The man swam up from beneath her and almost bumped into her as he surfaced. He was in snorkeling gear and had been using it to dive. Eve thought he must have come from the other side of the promontory, the place where Mike had warned her not to go. He swam by her, heading toward the beach. Eve thought he looked like the man she had seen earlier that day in the bar with Addison.

She watched him take off his gear as he walked up the beach and headed for a towel that was some distance from where she had left hers. She still had not gotten a good look at him, but now she was beginning to wonder if he might have been a tourist from the other cruise ship. That would explain why she had not seen him before, but it still did not explain how he happened to know Addison.

A moment later, Eve sensed someone else swimming near her. When she turned, she saw Tony swimming around the promontory with Addison close behind him. Addison surprised her with his friendliness.

"They sent me out to get you. I think it's time for lunch," he said.

Eve thought if they had really sent him for her, it was strange that he was coming from the wrong direction, but she said nothing about it. Tony, who did not appear to be a great swimmer, waved and continued to stroke toward shore using something resembling a dog paddle.

"I'll be right in," Eve said brusquely. She did not want to appear too friendly to Addison.

Addison hesitated. "The snorkeling is quite good, isn't it?" he said.

Eve wondered how he knew about how the snorkeling was when he wasn't wearing a mask or fins. Again, she did not question him about the inconsistency. Instead, she said, "There's so much to see that my curiosity gets the best of me, and I tend to lose track of time."

Addison's expression changed quickly, and she detected an unfriendly glint in his eye.

"Curiosity sometimes can be a dangerous thing," he said. Without another word, he began swimming toward shore.

Eve shuddered. She took his words as a warning to mind her own business and to stay out of whatever was happening. For a moment, she had almost dared to feel a little more friendly toward Addison. Now, she disliked him even more than she had in the first place, and she also distrusted him. She considered the possibility that the three were involved in something illegal. Drug smuggling was common in the Caribbean. So were arms sales and human trafficking.

Before heading for shore, Eve decided to swim to the end of the promontory to see what was on the other side and why Mike had warned her away. She decided that if as poor a swimmer as Tony could brave the currents, she should have no trouble. It took only a few minutes to round the point, and though Eve noticed a strengthening of the current, it was merely a gentle tug. She found nothing more menacing than a deserted white beach on the other side where she guessed the men must have met to converse privately. She wondered if that was why Mike had warned her away. Perhaps he too was a party to whatever was going on and his friendliness toward her was simply a facade. What better vehicle for smuggling than a cruise ship?

When Eve swam back to where the other passengers were lounging, she found they were already eating lunch. She looked for the stranger, but he had disappeared. Eve did not see him in the water, and as far as she could tell, no boats had picked up passengers. She guessed he had left by the narrow path that led into town.

Addison was propped up on one elbow on a towel about twenty feet from where Tony sat talking with his wife. He was pretending to read a book, but Eve saw his eyes flicker toward Tony's back. Both men again acted as if they were strangers.

The crew had set up a table under a tree, and two cooks were fixing hamburgers on a large grill that stood a few feet away. Once more, lunch was typical American fare. Eve longed for something more exotic than hamburgers and potato salad, but she did not want to leave the beach to walk to town. She planned to do more snorkeling after lunch. She would have plenty of time to sample the island restaurants during the remainder of the cruise, she told herself.

In the afternoon, Eve snorkeled around the promontory again. This time the beach was not deserted. She recognized two men from the *Clipper* who had spread towels on the beach and appeared to be in deep conversation. She thought one was called Ridge, but she hadn't been formally introduced. As she swam nearer, they picked up their towels and quickly headed into the brush and rocks that separated the two beaches. Someone else who didn't want company, she thought. She was beginning to feel unwelcome.

The beach, which was now deserted, was beautiful and quiet. Eve lay down on the white sand and promptly fell asleep. When she awoke, she could tell it was getting late. She was about to start back when she saw someone waving at her from atop the rocks between the two beaches. Mike was yelling something she could not understand.

A few minutes later, the launch appeared around the end of the promontory with Mike and two crewmen.

"We thought we'd lost you," Mike said, worry and annoyance giving an edge to his voice. "The rest of the passengers have already gone back, and the ship's about to sail. We got your stuff from the beach, but we couldn't find you."

"I'm sorry, I fell asleep," Eve said. "How'd you know I was here?"

"Luckily, Jerry Addison told us he thought he saw you swim out this way."

So good old Jerry was keeping an eye on her, too. It was not a pleasant thought.

It was nearly six o'clock when they got back to the ship, which had been scheduled to sail an hour earlier. Eve was embarrassed when the captain met her as she climbed aboard. "Is this going to become a regular occurrence?" Engstrum asked. Then he smiled. "We're glad you weren't hurt. Perhaps you should stay closer to the group when you swim; the currents can be deadly."

There was that *d* word that Irene liked so much, Eve thought, unwillingly remembering her warning about Sunday and the full moon.

Eve pushed the unpleasant recollection from her mind, blushed, and repeated her apology for making everyone late again.

She headed for her cabin to shower and change, hoping everyone would soon forget that she was once more the cause of the ship's late departure. As she passed the bar on her way to the stairs, she saw Addison sitting on a stool sipping a drink. He was looking at her with an odd expression on his face. If she was not already sure he didn't know how, Eve would have guessed it was a twinge of a smile.

Mike knocked on her door about ten minutes later to let her know the ship was about to leave port and something was about to happen on deck that she did not want to miss. She pulled on her other pair of shorts and the T-shirt she had bought at Melinda's shop, ran a brush through her hair to get rid of the snarls, and headed for the upper deck.

The passengers had already hoisted the Jolly Roger, and the first mate, Charlie Clark, a young Englishman with a cockney accent, was fussing with a small brass deck cannon that was mounted on the railing. "I think it's ready, sir," he said to Engstrum.

The captain scanned the sea and the rapidly closing distance between the *Sun Clipper* and the much larger cruise ship that still lay anchored in the harbor. The boats were so close now that even without straining her eyes, Eve could see that many of the cruise-ship passengers were seated at tables in what appeared to be the dining room.

The excitement aboard the *Sun Clipper* was mounting by the minute. A plump, red-faced dentist from California named Albert White could hardly contain his enthusiasm. "Now, now!" he yelled.

The captain raised his hand. "Fire!" Engstrum shouted. The cannon boomed loudly, and Eve thought the recoil might tear it from the railing. A moment later, a second cannon boomed. "Prepare to surrender your ship," Engstrum roared into a megaphone. "Prepare to board," he told the assembled *Sun Clipper* passengers.

His commands were answered by bursts of laughter and howls of delight from the *Sun Clipper* passengers, who were enjoying the havoc they were creating on the other cruise ship. Passengers on the larger vessel could be seen jumping from their chairs and running onto the deck to find out who was firing on them.

The other ship's captain, accustomed to the antics of the passengers on *Sun Clipper* cruises, responded with two ear-splitting blasts on the ship's horn as the *Clipper* headed toward the open sea.

"They're blanks," Mike said, pointing to the small cannons. He had come up beside Eve, who was still watching the other ship, where passengers continued to mill around on deck to get a better look at the *Clipper.* "We're running short of powder. We'll have to get more at one of the islands," he said. "The passengers love it. Makes them feel like they're real pirates." He laughed.

"I can see. I guess it doesn't matter how old one gets; we're all juvenile delinquents at heart," Eve said. She had to admit, the cruise was turning out to be more fun than she had expected.

CHAPTER SIX

Darkness comes quickly and without much warning in the tropics. It had fallen like a shroud over the ship before the second shift of diners had finished eating. Eve had barely touched her food, though she was hungry. The cook had made "roast beast" as the passengers referred disparagingly to the roast beef. She heard some complain it was the third time they had had some form of beef in as many days. Not much of a meat-eater, though no vegetarian, Eve decided she would eat in town at the next opportunity.

She was seated at a table with Mike and the nurses. He had introduced them to her as Cheryl, Linda, Melanie, Ulrika, and Candy. Nobody bothered much with last names, and Eve was glad because she was bad with names, not a particularly desirable attribute in a reporter. It was a matter of concentration or, in her case, lack of it. She tended to begin analyzing the personalities and traits of the individuals she met and forgot to concentrate on their names. With the nurses, it was enough not to mix up their first names without trying to learn their last names. Candy, short for Candace, turned out to be Mike's redheaded friend.

Though the nurses were sharing cabins, they were not from the same hospital or even the same cities in Canada and had not known each other before the cruise. They all belonged to the same travel club that had booked their tickets. Ulrika, who spoke with a heavy German accent, explained they had been members of the tour group for a long time and were usually paired up with other nurses on their vacations.

"Vee are all single. Zis vay ve get zee cheaper double occupancy rate," Ulrika explained.

"But you have only five," Eve said.

"Actually, there are six of us, but Justine has been sick almost since the beginning of the cruise," Candy said. "She gets seasick, and medication hasn't seemed to help much. On top of that, she got too much sun yesterday."

"She must be wishing she'd stayed home," Eve said. Candy and the others nodded in agreement.

"Who is the new guy?" Candy asked, abruptly changing the subject.

Eve had to turn in her chair to see who had caught Candy's attention. To her surprise, she saw the mystery man from the bar in Bequia, sitting at a table on the other side of the dining room. He glanced in their direction, colored slightly, and looked away when all the women at the table turned to look at him.

"Oh, his name's John Emory," Mike said. "He came aboard in Bequia. He'd been on another cruise, which he said wasn't much fun. He got off in Bequia and decided to join our cruise when he found out we had extra space."

That seemed odd to Eve, especially in light of his meeting with Addison in Bequia. "Do you usually pick up passengers during the cruise?" she asked.

"It happens occasionally but not very often," Mike said. "Most people sign up for either one or two weeks, and the majority take the two-week package. The same goes for other cruise lines. Most people don't jump ship. But if you're not having fun…" His voice trailed off as he studied Emory.

"He must be rich," Ulrika mused. "You can't get a refund in ze middle of a cruise."

"More important, is he married?" Cheryl asked, less interested in why he was here than in his availability. The other nurses giggled.

"I don't know much about him," Mike said. "I didn't even know he was here until the captain mentioned we'd picked up another passenger in Bequia. Kind of makes us sound like Greyhound of the islands." The nurses laughed politely at Mike's attempt to be funny and continued staring at John Emory, who glanced back and then tried to ignore them.

Eve scanned the room to see if any of the other players from the afternoon were there. Addison sat at the table next to theirs, but there was no sign of Tony or Flo. Emory was at a table with the Overtons, who looked even paler in the dining-room light than they had in the sunlight, and three other passengers whom Eve had seen before but had not yet met. John Emory looked uncomfortable, and he seemed to be watching the stairs that led to the cabins below. Perhaps he was waiting for Tony, Eve thought.

More intriguing to her was that Emory wasn't sitting with Addison, whom he obviously knew, but didn't want anyone else to know he knew. Neither gave the other any sign of recognition. Eve wondered why she seemed to be the only one who noticed that something odd was going on. Mike seemed oblivious to everything except the nurses, and the nurses were entertaining themselves by discussing Emory's dark, good looks and firm body.

"He's got great buns," Cheryl said mischievously. "I checked him out on the beach today."

"He's not bad looking either," Melanie quipped, and everyone laughed.

"I like his curly hair," Candy said. "Not bad pecs either. His nose is a little big, but you know what they say about men with big noses. I bet he's good in the sack." The laughter grew louder.

"You stay out of this one," Melanie admonished. "You've already got someone," she said, speaking as if Mike were not there.

Candy made a face at her. "You can never have too many," she replied, grinning and openly baiting Mike, who appeared embarrassed by the kind of repartee he was more accustomed to hearing in a men's locker room.

"Why don't you go after Addison again," Candy said. "Find out what his problem is."

"No, thanks," Cheryl said. "I don't think any of us are that desperate. He's not bad looking, but he's really an unfriendly jerk. Won't even talk or buy anyone a drink."

"Maybe he's, you know, one of them," Candy said, making a limp wrist motion. They all laughed uproariously.

"You're terrible," Mike interjected. "He probably just wants to be alone. Maybe he's got someone he really cares about at home."

"If he's got someone he cares about, why would he leave her at home and go on a romantic cruise by himself?" Candy asked, her mood becoming more somber as she studied her hands.

Eve noticed a light-colored circle around Candy's left ring finger that had not yet been eradicated by her tan, and she wondered if some of Candy's sexual pursuits and banter were attempts to cover a recent painful split.

"Well, maybe he's getting over someone. Besides, he's supposed to be working this trip. He's a journalist, you know," Mike said.

Candy turned to Eve. "Maybe you know what the scoop is with him," she said, returning to her previous light-heartedness. "You arrived with him, and you're a writer too, aren't you?"

"He doesn't talk to me either. In fact, I think he still hates me because I made him late getting to the ship by losing my luggage. Silly me."

The conversation, which centered around the availability of any of the single men on the ship, including the captain and other members of the crew, continued throughout the meal as Eve guessed it had at most meals since the beginning of the nurses' cruise more than a week ago. She judged their ages to range from midtwenties to midthirties, and none wore wedding bands.

So far, Candy, by far the most attractive of the group, with her beautiful red hair, white skin, and slightly voluptuous figure, was the only one to capture a man. Though Eve rather doubted Mike was a permanent catch. He struck her as someone who liked his freedom.

After dinner, Eve went for a walk around the deck. There was still no sign of Tony or Flo, which she found odd. In fact, she did not remember seeing them from the time she had returned to the ship. They were not among the passengers on deck when they fired the cannons. At least she had not seen them. Maybe they had decided to stay in their cabin for the evening and had ordered dinner brought down, Eve thought.

The night sky was full of stars, and the reflection of the moon shimmered silvery-white on the water. The air was heavy, and Eve thought she caught the smell of jasmine wafting on the breeze. She soon forgot about the Masons as she leaned against the railing sipping a rum punch and absorbing the beauty of the night. This was heaven and just what she had envisioned the cruise would be like when she was fighting with Wally for vacation time. She thought again of Irene, her superstitions and of the full moon that hung in the night sky. Wrong again, she thought.

The *Clipper*'s next stop, weather permitting, was supposed to be a deserted island in the Grenadines known for its beautiful reefs and outstanding snorkeling. Mike had said larger cruise ships usually passed by it because the reefs made it impossible for them to get close enough to land. Even on the *Clipper*, the island required a wet landing. Passengers were ferried in close to shore and then made to wade the rest of the way. She thought it sounded like it would be a great place to spend a quiet day.

Eve had lingered on deck for more than an hour after everyone appeared to have gone below and was heading for the stairs when she caught the sound of a man's voice coming from the shadows.

"It will all be over soon," he said. "Don't worry so much. Nobody's going to know. We've covered our tracks." The response was murmured and unintelligible. Eve hurried toward the sound of the voices and glimpsed Ridge and the other man from the beach descending the stairs to the lower deck.

Damn, Eve thought, there's more intrigue on this ship than at a city council meeting. Eve also went below. The noise level in the bar had risen, and the sound system was belting out some of Harry Belafonte's Caribbean hits. Mike and the nurses were drinking with several of the other passengers, but there was still no sign of Tony or Flo. While she was on deck, she had seen Addison and Emory each stroll once around the deck at separate times. But neither stayed in view for long, and now there was no sign of them either.

Several men had started playing cards at one of the tables. She saw the plump dentist, Dr. White, one of the leading delinquents during the cannon "attack," seated at the table. He was sipping a rum and Coke and smoking a huge cigar, while he played penny-ante poker with two crewmen and two passengers. Each time he dealt a card, he snapped it for emphasis as he placed it on the table. His red face was even more flushed than it had been in the afternoon, and Eve doubted the heightened flush was as much due to too much sun as to the amount of alcohol he had consumed.

During the shooting of the cannons, White had been wearing white shorts with hearts all over them that looked like underwear. Eve wondered if he had worn them to town; she did not remember seeing him on the beach. She smiled at the effect he would have had on the locals who may have thought they had seen everything in tourist attire until he arrived. Now, he was more conservatively dressed in blue shorts and a *Sun Clipper* T-shirt, similar to the one Eve had bought at the ship's store.

Eve watched the game for a few minutes and then drifted over to the bar for another drink before bed. She listened to Mike expound about previous cruises and the other ships of the line as he sipped beer from one of the largest mugs she had ever seen. A number of passengers had taken barefoot cruises before, a few on the *Sun Clipper,* which they loudly proclaimed the best of the line. For one thing, it boasted hot water, which some of the others did not have, they said. It was also the most beautiful, having at one time belonged to a wealthy financier. They also were on it now, which gave them bragging rights, Eve thought with some amusement.

The 236-foot ship was beautiful. Built in the 1930s, its interior walls were of polished mahogany and teakwood. The railings and fittings were shiny brass. When the sails were raised on the 132-foot-high mast as they were in the cover picture on the line's brochure, it was truly a magnificent sight to see. The cruises gave the *Clipper*'s passengers a sample of how the richest people in America had lived and played. It was a heady experience and hard to believe one individual had been wealthy enough to own such an expensive toy.

It seemed that everyone was enjoying the cruise except for Jerry Addison, who should have been having a grand time, Eve mused. His trip was free.

CHAPTER SEVEN

It was after midnight when Eve left the partiers in the bar and headed wearily down the stairs to her cabin. Her long trip to Saint Lucia, lack of sleep the night before, and the day in the Bequia sun had caught up with her. Even her nap on the beach had failed to refresh her. She would have no trouble sleeping.

The corridor was dimly lit and empty. Her cabin was the last one on the left before the door that led to the crews' quarters. As she walked toward it, she tried to shake off a growing sense of unease, attributing it to the darkened hallway and the perils of her profession.

She was surprised to find the door ajar. None of the cabins locked from the outside, but she was sure she had pulled it closed when she left before dinner. She was not concerned about theft because she had nothing to steal—unless the thief was into *Sun Clipper* T-shirts. Nevertheless, she approached cautiously, wondering if someone might be waiting inside. As she pushed the door open, she became immediately aware of an unpleasant odor that made her want to retch. Even in the dark, she knew what it was. She had smelled it before at crime scenes. The odor of drying blood coupled with the stench of sweat and urine was peculiar to the bodies of people who had died violently. The smell always turned her stomach.

Holding back the urge to vomit, with shaking hand she switched on the light and was surprised and relieved to find the room empty. She would have blamed her sensory reaction on her state of exhaustion if it had not been for the hand wedged between the wall and the slightly opened bathroom door.

The hand had brightly painted nails, and the fingers were heavy with diamond-studded rings. The jewelry and nails looked familiar. Her heart beat wildly, and her legs shook as she approached the door, dreading what she feared she would find inside.

By now, she was swallowing rapidly. Stifling back an urge to be sick, she pushed against the door, which would not budge. Peering through the crack, she saw the reason it was stuck. Flo's body was crumpled against it, and propped against the shower wall with his legs spread out beneath his wife's body was Tony. His eyes stared vacantly toward the opening. Blood ran from a gaping hole in the center of his forehead, and more stained the front of his white shirt. Eve could see a black-edged hole through the left pocket in the area of his heart. Flo's head was turned toward her husband, and the back of her bleached hair was matted with blood.

Blood appeared to cover nearly every surface, most of it almost dry. Eve's analytical mind warred with her natural inclination to become hysterical and to run from the room. She stood motionless, fighting the urge to escape while she absorbed details of the scene. Tony had been shot at least twice. That was evident. Flo also appeared to have been shot more than once, judging by the blood that had congealed on her head and back. There was no weapon, not one that she could see. It was not a murder-suicide.

By the time Eve had concluded to her horror that the gray material mixed with blood spatter on the shower wall behind Tony was brain matter, probably from an exit wound, she could no longer hold back the bile that had risen into her throat. She turned and lost her last meal in the sink next to the bathroom door. She rinsed her face under the tap water that ran at a maddening trickle. Not bothering to dry off, she retraced her steps to the cabin door and stepped outside.

In the corridor, she drew in a deep breath and with effort overcame her urge to scream for help, realizing that she had already done enough to contaminate the crime scene. What was not needed was to have every passenger on the ship rush to the cabin and destroy any evidence that might remain. She knew she should secure the door, but all she wanted to do was to get as far away as possible and to seek help. The sooner the better because the killer might be nearby. After all, it was a small ship. Wrapping the bottom of her shirt around the handle, she pulled the door shut. If there were any fingerprints, it might be possible to lift them from the latch, since she had not touched it on her way in. But who would have the expertise to do it? They were in the Caribbean without a forensics team on board.

As she ran toward the stairs, she wondered who had jurisdiction on the open sea. Idiotically, the comfort of a call to 911 crossed her mind, and the silliness of the idea made her feel giddy. If she were to be of any use investigating what had happened, she had to pull herself together.

Clearly the deaths seemed more than a random act of violence. But what could be the motive to kill Flo and Tony? Robbery could be ruled out because Flo's expensive jewelry had not been taken. They could not have surprised a burglar because they had no reason she could think of to be in her room in the first place, and she had nothing worth stealing. Whatever the reason, jurisdiction may have been something the killer had taken into consideration. Otherwise, why hadn't the Masons been killed on one of the islands instead of on a ship crowded with passengers in the middle of the ocean? It was also strange that the shots had not been heard.

And why pick her cabin? Eve thought miserably. The trip had been jinxed from the start, and she thought of Irene's dire warning. She would never hear the end of this one. If she were inclined to feel sorry for herself, this would have been the perfect time, she mused.

Pushing aside her own discomfort, she hurried on knowing that she needed to concentrate on finding help. If the investigation were delayed and the investigator inexperienced, it would give the killer an edge.

Every detail of the scene in the cabin was indelibly etched in her mind. Tony had probably died instantly. Flo's death had been sloppier. She had lived long enough to try to pry the door open, but she had been unable to move her own weight out of the way. Eve guessed she had not lived very long.

Mike was still in the bar, sipping a beer, when Eve bounded up the stairs. She looked around to see who else was there, half hoping to find the captain. He had apparently left earlier, and no one in authority was still in sight. Making a decision, she grabbed Mike's arm.

"What's up?" he asked, looking up from the glass he was twisting in his hand.

"I need to see the captain," Eve said, trying to remain calm.

"He's gone to bed," Mike said, his speech slurring slightly. "You'll have to talk to him in the morning. If it's about your luggage, I called today, and they still haven't found it."

"It's not about my luggage, and this can't wait. Get him now."

"What's going on?" Mike asked, sensing the urgency in her voice but obviously reluctant to wake the captain. "Engstrum doesn't like being disturbed except for emergencies."

"Trust me, this is one," Eve said insistently.

"Then tell me what it is, and I'll decide."

"There are two dead people in my cabin," Eve blurted out.

"Are you sure?" he asked stupidly.

Her face was ashen. Despite his alcoholic haze, the realization began to dawn on him that Eve wasn't joking. She looked like she was about to burst into tears or to deck him with her fist.

Moments later, they were knocking at one of the forward cabins, and a red-eyed, grumbling Captain Engstrum, dressed only in a robe, eventually opened the door.

As Eve told him what had happened, Engstrum's eyes became immediately alert. She was grateful that he never questioned her veracity. Instead, he nodded his head as she spoke and, within a matter of seconds, had pulled on shorts and a shirt and was pounding down the stairs to the corridor below. Mike, who seemed to have sobered up considerably in the last few minutes, trotted after them.

Engstrum was about to touch the handle of Eve's door when she pushed his hand away and used her shirt to nudge the door open. The odor was even worse this time. The smell of blood and dead bodies was now mingled with the lost contents of her stomach.

Engstrum looked at her. "I got sick," Eve said. He nodded, and a hint of a smile played across his lips.

Flo's hand still protruded lifelessly from the opening to the tiny bathroom. Engstrum tried, as Eve had, to push the door open, but with no better luck. He gave up and peered through the crack. When he turned around, Eve noticed with some satisfaction that he looked quite white-faced and was swallowing rapidly.

"My God," he said.

Mike was standing in the cabin doorway, eyeing Flo's hand. He had not seen the bodies, yet he appeared to be fighting back the urge to be sick.

Engstrum looked deeply shaken. "Nothing like this has ever happened before," he said helplessly. "It looks like they were shot."

"Oh, they were shot all right and at close range. You can see the powder burns on Tony's forehead and shirt."

"Someone would have heard the shots," Engstrum reasoned.

"Maybe they used a silencer. That could be why no one heard anything. I think it happened shortly after we left the island. The blood is coagulated but not completely dry," Eve said, surprised at her own ability to remain analytical in the presence of such carnage. "It would have taken longer to dry because of the humidity. It's quite damp because the clothes I rinsed out didn't dry overnight."

She hesitated and, after a pause, said slowly, "Possibly it happened while we were leaving port when most of the passengers were busy on deck."

"You think this happened while we were firing the cannons," Engstrum said, picking up on her line of thought.

"It would have been the perfect time. No one was below deck to hear or see anything, and the noise of the cannons and the shouting would have covered any sounds. If the Masons were killed while everyone was on deck, this also would explain why they were not at dinner. I know they were killed after we left because I showered before dinner, and I can assure you no one was here."

Engstrum seemed lost in thought while he pondered the latest revelation. Finally, he said slowly, "You mean you think the murderer is still on the ship?"

Of course, the killer had to be here. The ship hadn't stopped anywhere since leaving Bequia, and all the passengers had been on board before they left port. They always took a count to make sure. The prospect of having the killer nearby was something the captain did not want to think about. For an instant, Eve thought she detected fear in his eyes.

"No one's left the ship since we sailed, have they?" Eve asked.

"No, but maybe someone came on board while we were in port and hid until everyone was on deck. Maybe they swam ashore before we were clear of the harbor," Engstrum said hopefully.

"Someone would have seen them. It is not that easy to sneak onto a ship or to leave unseen when so many are watching from the deck," she said.

In fact, they must have been killed shortly after she left her cabin. She was sure of it. The thought of how close she had been to danger made her tremble. Thinking back, she remembered Mike had knocked at her door to tell her something was about to happen on deck. For a moment, she wondered if he might have been making sure no one was in the cabin so he could lure the Mason's to their death. But looking at him lurking in the doorway, fear written on his face, she doubted that he was a ruthless killer. He did not seem the type. Of course, some of the worst serial killers looked quite ordinary. It was possible he was a very good actor.

"And you think whoever did this is still on board?" Engstrum's repeated question interrupted her thoughts. She knew he was hoping for a different answer.

"He's got to be here unless he's a hell of a swimmer," Eve said, feeling sorry she could not provide a more comforting answer. "We probably should seal the room and notify the authorities. Do you know who has jurisdiction here?" she then asked, having regained her self-control.

"I don't think anyone does. What I mean to say is that I do; we're at sea. But I'm no detective," Engstrum said. Sorting out his options, he said, "I can radio for help. The nearest harbor where we could put in would be Green Parrot Cay. It's privately owned, but I don't think they have a police force, let alone a homicide investigator."

"Is there any way we could bring someone on board without going ashore?" Eve asked. "If my guess is right and the killer or killers are still on the ship, if we dock somewhere, they will have an opportunity to leave. That will make them much harder to catch."

Engstrum seemed to ponder this before speaking. "I suppose we could radio ahead and get either the authorities from Grenada or Saint Vincent to come on board."

Mike, the public-relations man who had worked so hard to make the cruise line successful, finally spoke. "If we do that, we could be tied up here for days. All the passengers will be held and questioned. I'm not sure that's in the cruise line's best interest."

"Do we have a choice?" Engstrum replied. Then almost to himself, he said, "Possibly, we do." He hesitated and then looked at Mike. "Get Emory. He's with some branch of the government—the FBI, I think. Maybe he will know what to do. Possibly he will know something about this. His presence here was supposed to be kept secret, but under the circumstances, I think we'll have to break that confidence."

Engstrum went on to explain that he had been radioed by Sinclair, the line's owner, just before the ship reached Bequia to expect another passenger. "Sinclair said it was most important that we cooperate with him in every way but not to disclose he was with the government. Sinclair didn't tell me why he was coming. I knew it was something official and never questioned it."

So that explained the unscheduled arrival of John Emory, Eve thought.

"If he's with the FBI, he should know what to do," she said, her spirits slightly lifted with the possibility that help might be at hand.

"Go wake him," Engstrum told Mike.

Glad to get away, Mike did not wait to have the order repeated; he hurried down the corridor toward Emory's cabin. Engstrum moved to the door to the crew's cabins and stepped inside. He grabbed the first crewman he came to, a man named Vincent who came from the island of Saint Vincent, and told him to stand guard at the door.

"Don't let anyone in or out without my permission," he said.

Vincent, who had been sleeping, sprang from his bunk and began pulling on his clothes.

Turning to Eve, Engstrum asked, "Do you think the other passengers are in danger?"

"There is no way to know, but somehow I doubt that whoever did this is planning any more murders. If I had done this, I would be figuring a way to get off the ship without being discovered. As long as no one else saw anything and as long as the killer doesn't feel threatened, I think the rest of the passengers should be safe. But there are no guarantees."

Engstrum looked down the dark corridor, and Eve could see his body stiffen. "Vincent, have Jerome help you stand guard, and call me if anyone tries to go near this cabin. Say nothing to the passengers or crew about this."

It took Vincent only a minute to return with Jerome, another Saint Vincent crewman. Eve could tell that both men were curious about why they had been roused from their beds to guard her cabin, but neither questioned the captain's order.

"It is most important that this door not be opened," Engstrum said.

A few minutes later, Mike returned by himself with the news that Emory wasn't in his cabin.

"Well, find him. He's probably in the bar or on deck," Engstrum said. "Bring him to my cabin when you do." After Mike left for the second time, Engstrum said, "You'd better come with me."

Eve didn't argue. Just then, the prospect of standing in the dimly lit corridor or sharing a cabin with two dead people held no appeal.

CHAPTER EIGHT

Once in Engstrum's cabin, which was massive in size compared to Eve's cramped quarters, the captain poured himself a drink from a decanter on the mahogany sideboard and offered her one. Eve declined, knowing that in order to handle whatever lay ahead, she needed to be in full control of her mental faculties. She was small, only about 110 pounds, and it did not take a lot to get her drunk. Right now, her stomach was empty, and she was very tired.

The captain's quarters must have been the stateroom of the previous owner. The main room was paneled in dark mahogany and furnished in heavy carved furniture, the kind found in the offices of outrageously expensive lawyers. A large desk covered with charts and maps filled one end of the room. The desk and some of the tables had tiny brass railings around the tops to keep things from sliding off in rough weather. Through a door, Eve could see a bedroom with an ornately carved mahogany bed. Yes, it was a little more luxurious than her tiny cabin.

Engstrum, an early forties no-frills type who stood before her in his bare feet, seemed out of place in the ornate setting. A former military man, he had an erect carriage and wore his close-cropped light-brown hair neatly trimmed. Despite a certain stiffness in appearance, Eve saw a gentler side of his personality mirrored in the sad hazel eyes that now watched her from across the room. He walked to the desk and pushed the maps out of the way to make room for his glass. His hand shook, causing the ice to clink. The unflappable captain who had distinguished himself in wartime, judging by the medals displayed on his uniform at dinner, was shaken by what was happening on his ship. And for a moment, Eve wondered how a man with his gentle demeanor could ever have killed anyone, even in battle. But the journalist in her quickly reminded her that looks were deceiving and some of the kindest-looking people were often the deadliest.

"I can't understand what's taking him so long to find Emory. The ship's not that big," Engstrum said, beginning to pace back and forth. She wondered if he thought movement would help him to gain control of the situation.

Eve considered telling him that perhaps they should look in Addison's cabin, but she thought she would wait until later to fill him in about the meetings she had witnessed. Right now, she wanted to know more about why an FBI agent had been brought aboard the ship.

"Did the owner tell you the reason Emory was being sent here?" Eve asked.

"No," Engstrum replied. "I believe it was routine. He was to get off somewhere south, I think. The phone connection was very bad. I'm not sure Sinclair knew why Emory was coming aboard."

"My experience as a reporter who has covered the feds tells me that the FBI wouldn't send an agent to the Caribbean if it were just routine," Eve said. "For one thing, they don't have jurisdiction here. They handle domestic crime. If the FBI were working a case here, it would almost have to be with the cooperation of one of the local governments. If any branch of the US government were involved in something here, you would think it would be the CIA or DEA. Are you sure he isn't with one of them?" Eve asked, wondering how familiar Engstrum was with the workings of intelligence agencies.

"He said FBI. I'm quite sure about that," Engstrum replied. "I wouldn't have misunderstood."

"What do you know about Tony and Flo?" Eve asked.

"Not much. Their surname is Mason. They're from Chicago. We don't do background checks on our passengers," he said dryly. "Maybe we should start."

"His last name is Mason, but somehow he doesn't look like a Mason," she said half to her herself. "Do you know what Tony does—I mean 'did'—for a living?" Eve asked.

"Said he was in sales. Shoes. Yes, that's it. He said he had a store," Engstrum said.

"And Flo, did she work?"

Engstrum shook his head. "I don't know. For all their chatter, they really didn't say much worth hearing. I admit I tuned out most of what they said. I know they had grandchildren. Flo told everyone the clothing she bought was for them. I'm sorry; I simply don't know anything about them that would make someone want to kill them. And, if I may ask, what is a Mason supposed to look like?"

Eve blushed at the sarcasm in his voice. "I just thought it odd that he had a Bronx accent, yet he said he was from Chicago and that his name was Mason when he looked like it should have ended in a vowel."

"My God, aren't there dark-skinned Masons in America? Aren't you making something of nothing?" Engstrum sounded both imperious and annoyed. "I never noticed Tony's accent, but then, I didn't grow up in the United States. I was an army brat. My dad moved us all over the world. Are you saying the poor devil was from New York and not Chicago? And you think he is of Italian heritage and traveling under an assumed name? That sounds farfetched. I can assure you, Mason is the name on his passport."

Not wanting to get into an argument by pointing out that passports can be forged, Eve helped herself to a glass of water from a pitcher on the sideboard next to the decanter and sat down in one of the heavy chairs. Reclining amid the thick cushions, she suddenly felt an overwhelming urge to go to sleep in a safe place and forget the horrible scene in her cabin. She certainly didn't want to return to her room to get the rest of her meager belongings. Exhaustion was starting to make her mind play tricks, and for a moment, all she could think about was having to buy more new clothes at the ship's store and wondering if the next purchases might exceed the limit on her Visa. She had to get some sleep before long.

"Why do you suppose they chose your cabin?" Engstrum asked.

"I have no idea," Eve said uncomfortably. She had been asking herself the same question ever since she had found the bodies. She hoped Emory would be able to answer some of their questions, including that one, once Mike found him.

"Are there any doctors on board besides Dr. White?" Eve asked.

"Usually we have several on each cruise. This time we have lawyers, but White's the only doctor," Engstrum said. "And he's not a doctor; he's a dentist." Eve was already quite aware of this, and wondered if the red-faced, middle-aged gentleman would remember enough of his anatomy classes to be of any help.

"We're going to need someone with medical expertise to examine the bodies, and he may have to do it if we can't find anyone else soon," Eve said. "One of the nurses could help, I suppose. And we also will need someone to take pictures of the crime scene before anything can be moved. Nearly everyone on board has a camera; it's just a matter of finding someone who can be trusted," Eve hesitated, "and someone who could not possibly be a suspect."

"I can't believe one of the passengers is a killer," Engstrum said, shaking his head. "But it would be even harder to believe one of the crew had committed such a terrible crime." He thought a moment longer and then suggested that Mike take the pictures. "He's got a camera, and he's had some training."

"That's good," Eve said. "I don't suppose anyone in your crew knows how to dust for prints? Is there a police officer on board?" she asked, surprised she hadn't thought to ask sooner.

Engstrum shook his head. "No one but Emory," he said.

When Emory was found, Eve expected he would know how to lift fingerprints if they could find what he needed. But Eve doubted he would find any. She was beginning to believe that whoever had killed the Masons had planned their deaths very carefully and would not have left anything as telling as fingerprints at the crime scene.

"We'll have to find a cool place to store the bodies to preserve them for an autopsy if we are not going into port right away," Eve said.

Engstrum nodded. A former naval officer, he was well aware of what the heat in the tropics would do to bodies that were not refrigerated. "I suppose we could put them in one of the food lockers. It's the only place large enough and cold enough."

Eve had a visual picture of the bloody bodies lying next to the roast beast, and once more she felt as if she were about to lose what little supper might have been left in her stomach. She swallowed several times, and the nausea subsided.

Though it seemed much longer, only fifteen minutes had passed when Mike knocked at the door. "It's open," Engstrum said.

Mike's face was pale. "I can't find him anywhere. I've looked everywhere except in the passengers' cabins. I didn't know if you would want me to wake everyone up at this hour. It could start a panic," he said. "He's not in his cabin; he's not on deck or in the crews' quarters. Unless he's in someone's cabin, he's not on board."

"Impossible," Engstrum snapped. "No one's left the ship since we got underway. I saw him at dinner. Check the cabins. Take a couple of the crew with you, but don't tell them what's going on.

Just say I've got an urgent message for Emory. Tell the passengers the same thing. No point in alarming them."

Mike left without another word. He still appeared pale as a ghost, and Eve suspected he probably had a hangover, but he was no longer drunk. It was amazing how sobering the sight of blood could be—unless his alcoholic daze in the bar had been an act. She wondered.

CHAPTER NINE

Engstrum got up from behind his desk and paced the floor. Usually a man of action, he was feeling both restless and helpless.

"We could help," Eve said.

"I was thinking the same thing," he said. "No point in sitting here."

Once in the dark passageway, it took only a few moments for them to catch up with Mike and the others. Within a half hour, they had knocked on every cabin door, awakening nearly everyone on the ship, but Emory had not been found.

Puzzled, Engstrum led Eve and Mike back to his quarters. He dispatched the other crew members to search the rest of the ship a second time just to be sure Emory had not left his cabin to take a walk on deck after they had begun their search below deck.

"If we don't find him, I'm going to have to radio Sinclair. I don't relish getting him involved, but he can get hold of whoever contacted him to get Emory on board."

It was after 2:00 a.m., and hardly anyone was on deck. The bar was closed, and even the diehard drinkers had straggled off to bed. Eve doubted that Emory would be found on deck during the second search. She was beginning to doubt he would be found at all. He was not in any of the cabins unless he was hiding...or being hidden, Eve thought. Perhaps he had gone overboard, either willingly or by force, but why hadn't anyone heard a splash? And no lifeboats were missing.

Again, she thought of the strange meetings she had witnessed in Bequia. She was not ready to draw attention to Addison yet, but since he appeared to be the only one left of the three who was still available and able to talk, Eve knew she would have to tell Engstrum about him soon. Maybe he would be able to shed some light on the situation. Eve also wondered if Addison might have been the person who had lured Tony and Flo to her cabin and then killed them. His cabin was next to hers. It would have been convenient to have taken them there, killed them, and then slipped into his own cabin without being seen. She shuddered at the thought.

There was definitely a link between Addison and the dead Masons. But another Bequia meeting and the odd conversation she had overheard the night before between Ridge and the man she had later learned was Edward Amsterdam came back to her.

"It will all be over soon," Ridge had said. Could he have been talking about the lives of Flo and Tony? What did he mean when he told Amsterdam not to worry because they had "covered their tracks"? Why hadn't they wanted anyone to see them together on the beach in Bequia?

And what about Emory, and for that matter Sinclair? The only word on Emory's being an FBI agent had come from Sinclair, a man she knew nothing about. What if Emory weren't really an FBI agent at all? The FBI didn't usually work outside the United States. What if he had come to kill Tony and Flo and then had found a way to get off the ship? And what if the mysterious Sinclair had set the whole thing up? But why? Obviously, the key lay in knowing more about Tony and Flo and the murder itself.

When she thought about the murders, one word came to mind: neat. They were marched into a shower and shot, and even most of the blood ran down the drain. As a reporter, Eve had found that most random murders were committed by rather ordinary criminals who weren't neat. Most killings were messy, ill conceived, and the killer left clues. This killer hadn't even gotten blood on the carpet, at least none that she had seen.

Questions and theories about the murder filled her mind. She still hadn't ruled out the possibility that the motive was as simple as burglary or theft. Tony and Flo had certainly flaunted the fact that they had money, buying everything they could lug back to their cabin. But if theft were the motive, wouldn't Flo's enormous diamond rings have been the first to go? They were still on her ring finger. Eve had seen them on her extended hand. It would be easier to determine if money was missing once they searched their bodies, clothing, and cabin. Missing money would indicate theft as a motive, though Eve would still have a problem accepting that a thief would overlook such valuable jewelry. She also reasoned that most of the cruise-ship passengers, with the possible exception of the reporters, seemed to be fairly well off. Maybe jealousy was the motive…or blackmail. Maybe the Masons were blackmailers or extortionists, and someone had killed them for that reason.

And was the killer after Tony and Flo or just one of them? Who would want to kill Flo? she asked herself. The only person she could think of was Tony, a husband tired of her extravagance. But that would not explain who had killed him. Maybe something would turn up in their past that would make her the target and Tony the dupe who just happened to be with her. More likely it was Flo who was in the wrong place at the wrong time, she thought.

Eve's mind turned back to Jerry Addison. She didn't like him or trust him, but that did not make him a killer. He definitely knew Tony and may have been one of the last people to have talked to him—or argued with him—before he died, she thought. During the cabin check, she had watched as Mike had knocked at Addison's cabin door. After a couple of minutes, Addison had reluctantly opened it. He was wearing pajamas and appeared to have been sleeping. He was irked at being disturbed and had been quite unpleasant, demanding to know what was going on. He did not appear satisfied with Mike's explanation about the message for Emory.

"You'd think something like that could wait until morning!" he'd barked before slamming the door in Mike's face.

Eve's thoughts were drawn back to Engstrum, who was looking anxious and was again pacing the floor. Now he suggested wearily that perhaps they should search the showers, since they had not done so during their previous cabin checks.

"What reason would we give the passengers?" Mike asked. "Telling them that we have an urgent message for Emory, and we need to search their showers isn't going to work."

For the first time that night, Engstrum smiled. "You're right, of course. Besides, I can't imagine if he were hiding in someone's shower that they wouldn't know about it."

"Unless he's dead too or being held," Eve said. Engstrum stopped smiling.

Minutes later, one of the crewmen knocked at the door to inform Engstrum that Emory had not been found during their second search of the decks and the crews' quarters. Engstrum excused him and told him to go to his quarters and await further orders. No one was going to get much sleep that night.

"I'd better radio Sinclair," Engstrum said. Eve and Mike followed him to the small room that held the radio equipment. It was the only room on the ship that had not been searched because it was kept locked when it was not in use. Engstrum started to insert his key into the lock when Eve stopped him.

"I think you'll find the door is open," she said.

Engstrum looked startled and pushed at the narrow wooden door, which swung open, banging against the wall.

"You can see that it's been forced," Eve said, stepping aside to let the full light from a deck lantern fall on the splintered wood around the lock.

Engstrum drew a sharp breath as he stepped through the doorway and viewed the carnage inside. The radio had been pulled from the wall and completely dismantled. Bits of wires and parts were strewn on the floor. The satellite phone was missing. The cell phones that had been collected from the passengers were gone too. There would be no way to radio the home office in Miami, the FBI, or anyone else. The killer had seen to that.

"Even if all the parts are still here, which I doubt, it could take days to put this thing in working order," Engstrum said, sighing deeply. "We'll just have to put in at the nearest port and take our chances with the locals. I see no other choice. Now we can't even call for a pilot when we reach port. We'll have to get close enough to shore to put the launch down."

"What about cell phones?" Eve asked.

"Even if someone kept theirs when they were supposed to turn them in, you can't get reception of any kind out here," Engstrum said. "We're in a virtual dead zone. I've been trying to get the company to upgrade our communications equipment, but they didn't want to spend the money and wanted to keep the sailing experience on an old ship as authentic as possible. Admittedly, the old system has been enough until now."

Mike eyed the captain and the mess in the room. "I think we should talk this over before we bring in the local authorities. As I said before, if we do that, we could be looking at everyone on ship being detained for who knows how long. I know this may not be the time to be thinking about the bottom line, but you and I both know how hard Sinclair has struggled to keep the line going. It's only been in the last year that business has really picked up. It's bad enough that someone was killed here, but if the passengers are held for what could be days while the locals investigate the murders, we will not only have to refund everyone's money but also the line would be looking at a potential for lawsuits. Huge lawsuits—the kind that could sink this line for good."

Eve wondered if Mike might have another reason for wanting to delay involving the local police. Worrying about lawsuits and a cruise line's image seemed a bit lame with a killer on the loose.

"What you say is true, but what other choice do we have?" Engstrum asked. "None of us are detectives. By doing nothing, we could be endangering the other passengers. What if the killer strikes again? If you're worried about lawsuits, think about what happens if I do nothing and someone else is killed. Even if I could be sure everyone else were safe, I can't leave two bodies lying in that cabin indefinitely."

Eve noted that the captain refrained from saying her cabin, though he shot a glance in her direction, and she was reasonably sure she knew what he was thinking. She had been a jinx ever since she had come aboard. First, she had made the ship late leaving Saint Lucia and then Bequia, and now her cabin was the site of a double homicide.

"You are right," Engstrum continued, directing his statement to Eve, "if we move the bodies, we need to have them examined first. We need to take photos and collect fingerprints and do all the things a trained investigator would do. But we don't have the expertise. If we had found Emory, the situation would have been different."

Eve had been listening, but her mind was racing ahead. If the ship docked, the killer would escape. The only way to catch him was to keep him on board.

"Mike has a point," Eve heard herself saying. It was probably the first time she had agreed with much of anything he had said since she had joined the cruise. She generally had little respect for PR types and even less for womanizers. But in this instance, Mike's point was well taken. The local authorities would probably hold everyone for weeks because a very strong probability existed that the murderer was still on the ship. Even the least-experienced investigator would not allow his prime suspects to depart to different parts of the world far beyond his legal grasp. And that brought up the yet unanswered point. Who really did have jurisdiction?

"If I can make a suggestion..." Eve began.

"Please feel free," Engstrum said, gesturing resignedly with his hand. "I'm about out of ideas."

"Let's get Dr. White up and have him examine the bodies. The means of their deaths looks pretty straightforward, and even if it has been a long time, he did have some general medical training, which should help here. We could get one of the nurses to help, kind of as a backup, if White wants it. And, Mike, you should take pictures of the bodies and the crime scene. You're a professional photographer; you've got the equipment and the knowledge. Once the bodies have been examined and photographed, we can move them to that meat locker if we have to.

"We also need to search the cabin thoroughly and the corridor around it. We need to question anyone who was below deck about the time we believe the Masons may have been killed. After examining the cabin and the corridor, we'll need to seal the cabin and keep as many people out of the corridor as possible to preserve any evidence. We also need to search the Masons' cabin to see if we can tell if anything is missing. We'll seal it when we're through. In the meantime, we should probably try to get near enough to a port or a place to go ashore so that we can send in a launch without actually landing the ship. Whoever we send can phone the FBI and the Miami office for instructions."

Both Mike and Engstrum looked at Eve with some degree of respect. "That's good thinking," Mike said.

Engstrum nodded. "By morning we could be near enough to Green Parrot Cay to send a launch. The beauty of the cay is that it's privately owned, though I believe it might fall under the authority of Saint Vincent in matters of police business. But I know the owner. I think he'll be willing to help us without notifying the authorities until we're ready."

Eve also suggested that guards be posted on deck to make sure no one left the ship when it came closer to shore. Engstrum agreed.

"There is one other thing," Eve added. "Before we do anything, there are some things I think you should know."

It was time to tell the captain what she knew of Ridge, Amsterdam, and Addison and what she had seen on Bequia. They had left the radio room and were on deck. Eve leaned against the railing with her back to the sea. Mike and Engstrum stood watching and listening intently as she told of Ridge and Amsterdam's hasty retreat from the beach and the conversation she had later overheard on deck.

"What Ridge said sounded suspicious, but there could be a very logical and simple explanation for it that has nothing to do with murder," Eve said. Both men nodded, but neither said anything, waiting for her to continue.

She told them of the meetings between Emory, Addison, and Tony. As Eve talked, the moonlight reflected off the water, illuminating the anxiety in their faces. When she had finished, both men were silent. Finally, Mike spoke.

"You mean you think Addison may not be a journalist at all and that he may have had something to do with what happened to the Masons?"

"All I know is that I saw all of them together in Bequia, and they definitely knew each other, although it seemed they did not want anyone else to know it."

"I wonder if Emory might have been sent here to protect Flo and Tony?" Mike asked. "If he was, he didn't do much of a job."

"Or to kill them," Eve said. "We don't even know if he's with the FBI. And maybe Addison was an accomplice. We really don't know anything about him other than no one seems to like him."

Engstrum began walking toward the stairs. He turned when he reached the top. "I think I'll have a talk with Mr. Addison. I'll talk to Ridge and Amsterdam later. Care to join me?"

When they reached Addison's door, Engstrum knocked softly at first and then more loudly. No one answered. Without waiting, he tried the door and went inside. Eve followed, half afraid to see what she might find. The cabin was empty.

"Did you see Addison leave?" Engstrum asked Vincent, who was sitting in the corridor guarding the door to Eve's cabin.

"He got dressed and went up on deck after you knocked before," Vincent said.

Mike, Eve, and the captain all exchanged glances. Perhaps it was Addison who had wrecked the radio. It was also possible he had been listening while they were talking on deck.

"We need to find him. Maybe he knows what happened to Emory. He could have had something to do with his disappearance. Or perhaps they were working together, and they've both found a way to get off the ship," Engstrum said.

"If it were that easy to leave, the killer wouldn't have had to destroy the radio to buy time," Eve said. "No, I think whoever killed the Masons is still here."

While the captain and Mike looked for Addison, Eve decided to pay a wakeup call on Ridge and Amsterdam. They shared a cabin that was next to the one where Tony and Flo had spent their last days together.

It was Calvin Ridge who answered the door. He was a slim, wiry man with thinning gray hair that he brushed carefully over a bald spot. Now the piece of hair, tousled in sleep, hung shoulder length on one side of his head, leaving the shiny spot exposed. He would have appeared vulnerable if it had not been for his height and the penetrating black eyes that stared at her from under bushy brows. She felt uncomfortable.

"What do you want?" Ridge asked irritably.

That was a good question, Eve thought, looking past Ridge to catch a glimpse of Amsterdam asleep in the lower bunk. She wondered if someone who had just murdered two people would be able to sleep so peacefully. A normal person might never sleep comfortably again, but a cold-blooded killer probably wouldn't be bothered by a nagging conscience.

"I was wondering if you've seen Tony and Flo," Eve asked. She knew she should have planned her questions, but she hadn't had time, and this was the first one that came to mind. She watched for his reaction at the mention of their names but saw only anger registered in his eyes.

"What is going on tonight? Someone was just here asking if I had seen Emory. No, I haven't seen Tony and Flo or Emory," Ridge said. "I've been asleep. At least I've been trying to sleep. Edward can sleep through anything, but I can't. Now, I'm going to shut the door, and if anyone stops by looking for anyone else tonight, I'm going to complain to the captain," he said.

"Did you hear anyone in their cabin earlier?" Eve asked, ignoring his threat. "It's next to yours."

"No, as I told you, I was asleep, and I plan to go back to sleep." His hand found the stray lock and brushed it back across the top of his head. Then he closed the door and left her standing in the hall.

Vacation must be slowing me down, she thought. Usually between the time someone threatens to slam a door and when it actually happens, a good reporter can come up with more than one question.

As Eve backed away from the door, she found herself standing next to Flo and Tony's cabin. The urge to get a look inside before anything was disturbed overwhelmed her. She knew she should wait for the captain, but she wanted to be alone to think and to feel what may have been happening there before they died. She automatically raised her hand to knock but stopped in midair, knowing there was no one left to answer the door.

Inside, the cabin was as she had envisioned it would be. It had been Flo's realm. Tony appeared to have been only a visitor. Suitcases were piled high on a luggage rack in the corner. Shopping bags of clothing were heaped in a corner and on the lower bunk. She recognized several bags from Melinda's store. The small dressing table was strewn with cosmetics, nail polish, and perfume. A cosmetics case on the floor had caught an overflow of lotions and skin-care products that would not fit on the table. The hooks on the wall and on the door to the head bent under the weight of Flo's clothing. The tiny closet was stuffed beyond its capacity with dresses, blouses, and other feminine attire.

At first glance, the only sign that Tony had even shared the room with her was a razor and a small bottle of shaving cream pushed into a corner of the shelf above the sink. She wondered where Tony had kept his clothes. Even the dresser drawers contained only Flo's clothing. She looked at the stack of suitcases and suspected that Tony had been relegated to living out of one of them for the trip.

The bunks, though rumpled, had not been slept in. And it did not look as if the room had been searched, though it was hard to tell in the disarray. She had noticed Flo's purse on the closet floor. She pulled it out and opened it, carefully sorting through the contents, which included an assortment of cosmetics and combs. Eve slid her hand beneath the strip that served as the bottom of the purse and pulled out a wad of bills. They were in twenties and larger denominations. She guessed they would add up to thousands of dollars. Flo's credit cards were in a side pocket with her driver's license. If the motive had been theft, the killer had missed the mother lode, Eve thought.

She had replaced the money under the flap in the purse and was standing in the middle of the room when she was startled by the noise of the door latch being depressed.

"Who's there?" she called.

The pressure on the latch was immediately released, and Eve heard footsteps hurrying down the hall.

She ran to the door and flung it open, hoping to see who had been about to enter the cabin. Nearby, she heard a door close along the darkened corridor. He was here, she thought. Perhaps the killer had come for something that was in the room, and if she had kept quiet, she might have seen him. She might also have ended up dead. She wondered if the visitor might have been Calvin Ridge. His cabin was one of the closest.

It was imperative that the room be searched now before the visitor at the door could return. She ran down the corridor, but it still took her nearly fifteen minutes to find Mike and the captain and to return to the cabin. They still had not found Addison.

Eve's heart sank when she opened the door. Flo's purse, which she had returned to the closet, lay upside down on the floor, with its contents scattered. The wad of bills was gone.

"Perhaps robbery was the motive," Engstrum said, surveying the scene. "How much money was there?"

"I didn't count it. But it had to be several thousand dollars," she said.

Engstrum eyed her speculatively for a moment, and Eve wondered if he thought she had taken it.

"You say the purse was in the closet when you found it," he continued.

"Yes, and I put it back," she said.

"Why did you come here without waiting for us?"

She told him about her conversation with Calvin Ridge, of her subsequent urge to explore the cabin, and about the person who tried the door and ran away when she called out.

"Well, perhaps we should search the cabin thoroughly while we're here," he said, seeming to accept her explanation.

It took the three of them only a short time to go through the cabin and all of the murdered couple's belongings. There was nothing of particular interest. They found a few pictures of a smiling Flo with two adults and several small children. Eve guessed them to be her children and grandchildren. If there were few traces of Tony's presence in the cabin, evidence that he had been part of the family was nonexistent. He was absent from the family photos, a fact that Eve found odd.

"That about does it," Engstrum said, getting up from where he had been kneeling to examine the contents of the last suitcase.

"The missing money points to robbery as the motive," he said.

"Why would the thief have waited so long after killing them to rob them?" Eve asked. "And why leave the rings? Why kill them at all when you could rob them while they slept? It just doesn't make sense."

Engstrum was already on his way out the door when he turned. "Maybe they left the rings and went for the money because it would be harder to trace. The rings could lead the authorities right back to the victims. Anyway, if you've got a better theory than robbery, let's hear it."

Eve couldn't think of one. She was too busy second-guessing herself and wishing she had staked out the corridor or the cabin instead of going for help. She might know who the killer was by now. There would be no need for speculation.

CHAPTER TEN

After they finished searching the cabin, Mike and the captain returned to survey the communications room. The captain seemed determined to will the radio back to life.

Eve remained on deck alone with her thoughts. Both men had expressed concern at leaving her without protection, but she assured them she would be fine. She needed time to process all that had happened, and she could do that better by herself.

Leaning against the railing, she sifted through the events of the evening. Even after the theft of the money, Eve still doubted theft had been the motive for the murders. She had been suspicious that Tony was involved in something illegal and was in some kind of trouble ever since she had seen the three men together in Bequia, but she had been unable to figure out what it might be. She had certainly been right about his troubles.

At first, Eve had thought that Addison and Emory might be the reason for Tony's problems, maybe former business partners or loan collectors who were after him for nonpayment of a debt. Of course, that was before she learned Emory was supposed to be an

FBI agent. If it turned out that he was, it would certainly make it less likely that Emory was involved in a double homicide. If he were found, he might be able to supply a motive. Certainly, she would like to have the opportunity to ask him why he was here and what he knew about the Masons.

If Emory's supposed FBI status eliminated him, at least for the moment, from consideration as the possible killer, that left Addison as a prime suspect. What was his role in all this? By now, she was thoroughly convinced he wasn't a reporter, but that didn't make him a killer. She did not know where he fit into the puzzle.

Tony might have been involved in drug dealing or a gambler who couldn't pay his debts. The islands were known as conduits for drug trafficking between South America and the States. Eve knew the profit in drug sales was so high it had been known to corrupt all kinds of people, including members of law enforcement. Somehow Tony did not strike Eve as the type to be involved in drugs, although appearances often were deceiving. Moreover, she could more easily visualize Tony in the role of the compulsive gambler, but she had no idea why he struck her in this way. As far as she knew, he hadn't even joined in Dr. White's dining-room card games.

Even if Tony had been involved in something illegal and owed somebody money, most thugs who collected those kinds of debts were instructed to intimidate, not to kill, Eve reasoned. Dead men never repaid their debts. Murder was bad for business, and it brought unwanted police scrutiny. Besides, why would anyone, even the Mafia, send a thug on a Caribbean cruise just to collect a gambling debt? They could just as easily pressure Tony—and even dispense with him—when he got home. In the darkness, Eve shook her head.

Now she considered whether Flo had been the target. It seemed so unlikely. Eve couldn't remember anyone getting killed for exceeding their credit-card limit or wearing gaudy clothes. If Flo was involved in something sinister, nothing came to mind. It couldn't even be a case where Tony had insured her for a lot of money and then had her killed. He was dead too. Flo was the kind of woman who could easily make a rich man poor. But Tony had seemed devoted to his wife, and there was no way their deaths in her shower could be construed as a murder-suicide. She hadn't seen a weapon.

Turning back to Emory, she again tried to see where he might fit into the picture. What if he were an FBI agent who had become involved in something illegal? What if he had been corrupted by money and Tony knew about it and had threatened to expose him? Or what if he had been working under cover with Tony, and now he was dead too? As far as she knew, the FBI wasn't into collecting bad gambling debts, dealing illicit drugs, or engaging in murder for hire. But why was Emory here? Something had definitely linked the men together, of that she was sure. Perhaps Emory had been sent to protect Tony from someone, and maybe that someone was Addison. But why? And what if Emory were an imposter? It seemed the ship was full of them. Addison certainly wasn't what he had represented himself to be, and neither were the Masons. And obviously, someone on board was posing as a tourist when he was a murderer.

If only they could find Emory and question him. Whoever he was, he held an important key to the mystery. At least he might provide them with a reason for what had happened. He might know who wanted Tony and Flo dead badly enough to follow them to the Caribbean. But as time passed, Eve thought the chances of finding him were becoming slim. The ship was not that large, and there could not be that many hiding places. He was either dead, possibly thrown overboard, or he had found a way to get off the ship. It would be important to check Emory's credentials out at the earliest possible opportunity.

Now the remaining member of the Bequia trio was Addison. She doubted if they would get a straight story out of him, providing they even found him. They would be lucky to get him to be civil, let alone to answer any questions. One of the first things Eve intended to do if they ever got to a phone was to check on that travel magazine he said he worked for to see if it even existed. She kicked herself for not asking him more questions about it when they were on their way to the ship. But he had been so unfriendly, she had preferred chit-chatting with Mike. She had had no idea he would become the focus of a murder investigation. If they found him, she fully expected he would be as angry and abrasive as he had been when they had knocked at his door earlier.

No doubt he would be upset that someone had had the bad judgment to kill Flo and Tony, thus putting a further crimp in his vacation plans, Eve thought bitterly. Besides, he would probably find a way to blame it on her because the murders had happened in her cabin. She seethed at the thought of how she would react if he made one nasty remark about that. Suddenly, she realized how tired she was, a condition easily attributed to lack of sleep and the night's horrific events. She was holding onto self-control by a thread, and the minute he opened his mouth to make some snarky remark, she would punch him.

The full moon, which had temporarily gone under a cloud, once again bathed the deck with muted light. She stretched her tired body and was about to go in search of Mike and the captain when a shadowy figure stepped from behind the tall mast and walked toward her.

"Who is it?" she asked, hearing the tremor of fear in voice and feeling her heart beginning to pound in her chest. She had thought she was alone on deck. Apparently, she was wrong. Now, she calculated whether she could make a dash for the stairs before the figure reached her, but he was already too close. When he stepped into the moonlight, Eve drew in a sharp breath as she saw Addison move stealthily toward her. He held something in his hand, and the moonlight glinted off the shiny object long enough for Eve to see that it was a gun.

"Don't move," he said, his voice barely a whisper.

Eve froze where she was, as the trembling in her body increased until she was sure everyone on board would be able to hear her knees knocking.

"I won't tell anyone—" she started to say as he cut her off in midsentence.

"Shush," he said, putting a finger to his lips.

Eve's heart pounded, and she waited for him to shoot; but, instead, he moved past her, hardly making a sound. He disappeared behind a pile of rigging and left her standing in the middle of the deck, too frozen to move. A moment later, he reappeared on the other side and walked quietly toward her, shoving the gun into his waistband.

"I'm sorry I frightened you, but I thought I saw someone back there. I wanted to make sure. After what's happened, you shouldn't be here by yourself," he said. His voice was solicitous, and he put an arm around her trembling shoulders.

Eve felt herself sway and knew if she had been given to fainting, she would have swooned on the spot. Instead, she started to cry and immediately hated herself for allowing her emotions to get the better of her at a time when she needed all the control she could muster.

Addison hugged her awkwardly, his attitude completely changed from the abrasive man Eve had known. "It's all right," he said. "You've had a terrible night. You really ought to get some rest."

"I can't go to my cabin," Eve said, blubbering like a child.

"I know," he said. "If you want to, you can take mine for what's left of the night."

"You know what happened?" she asked, suddenly becoming suspicious again.

"Yes, I know," he said.

"Did you kill them?" Eve blurted out.

"Whatever gave you that idea?" Addison asked.

"You've got a gun, and how else would you know they're dead?"

Addison laughed. "Like you, I'm a trained investigator." Smiling at her shocked expression, he continued, "After Mike knocked at the door, I decided I had better find out what was really going on. I found Vincent guarding your door and got him to tell me. I had him let me take a look."

"He had orders not to let anyone into that room. He should never have let you in," Eve said, regaining some of her control.

"I had something that convinced him it would be a good idea," Addison said. "Now don't you think we ought to go below and talk to the captain? I understand all of you were looking for me."

CHAPTER ELEVEN

Addison never let go of Eve's arm as he led her to the captain's cabin. She had declined his invitation to let her use his cabin to get some rest. This did not seem to surprise Addison, and he didn't insist.

Captain Engstrum appeared relieved when they walked through his door. Though he did not say what he had been thinking, it was clear from the look on his face that he had feared Addison might also have disappeared or would be found dead. His look of relief changed, however, when he saw the gun. Addison had tucked it into the band of his shorts. Mike, who had been talking to Engstrum when they came in, grew silent and wary as he eyed Addison and the weapon.

"I think there are a few things you need to know," Addison began, before either of the other men could speak. He reached for something in his pocket, and both men jumped simultaneously, fearing he was reaching for the gun. A smile flickered across Addison's face as he observed their reactions. He pulled a small leather case out of his pocket and flipped it open on the captain's desk. It contained his badge.

"As you can see, I'm not really a writer. I'm with the federal marshal's service," he said. "In light of what's happened, I think you need to know what was going on here and why both Emory and I were aboard your ship." He paused a moment before continuing. Engstrum, Eve, and Mike were watching him intently.

"The man you know as Tony Mason was a protected witness, and I know what you are going to say. Obviously, we didn't protect him very well, or he and his wife wouldn't be dead now." Addison paused to let his words sink in.

"That would explain how you're carrying on a ship where it is not allowed," Engstrum said slowly, exhibiting a look that wavered between relief and anger. "You can tell me later how you got it through customs and on board. But first, I'd like to know what you know about the Masons and why they were on my ship. If they were in some kind of danger, it seems hardly the place to hide them. And while we're at it, you might let us know who wanted to kill them and how a killer got on board. Obviously, there are a lot of people with us who don't belong here," Engstrum said, directing an angry look at Mike, who merely shrugged his shoulders.

Addison sighed deeply and suddenly looked both tired and defeated. He seemed to be drawing on his last reserves to keep going. Eve was surprised to find herself feeling sorry for him. If his job had been to protect Tony, he'd blown it badly.

"I'll try to be brief," Addison said. "Tony was a high-ranking member of one of the major organized crime families on the East Coast. He ran some of their loan sharking and gambling interests. But in 1998, he was arrested by the FBI and charged with racketeering for his involvement in those activities. He was also charged with conspiracy to commit murder in the death of another mobster who had tried to squeeze Tony out of his territory," Addison said, pausing long enough in his narration to sit down in one of the well-cushioned chairs. Engstrum, who had been standing behind his desk, also sank down.

"Tony was looking at a sure conviction, probably on both charges, and a very long prison sentence. He hadn't exactly been an exemplary member of society. He had a prior record for armed robbery and felonious assault, among other things, and had spent a considerable amount of his adult life in prison. It was not a place he enjoyed. He was only forty years old and didn't find the prospect of spending the rest of his life in prison very appealing. He was approached by the FBI and offered a deal. In return for his cooperation and testimony against the mob in future trials, he would be given a break and allowed to plead to reduced charges. He would serve only a little time in jail and be placed in the witness protection program. He and his family would be moved out of town. They would be given new identities, new jobs, and Tony would be allowed to undergo plastic surgery to change his appearance. All of this, of course, at the taxpayer's expense."

"So what was he doing on my ship?" Engstrum interrupted irritably. "Does the program also pay for Caribbean cruises?"

"I'm getting to that," Addison said. "Tony agreed to the government's offer and kept his end of the bargain. He was allowed to plead to lesser charges and given credit for the time he had already spent in prison while awaiting trial. He really spent very little time behind bars because he was kept out in order to testify. His testimony was key to the prosecution of a number of organized crime bosses across the country because Tony was a fountain of knowledge, probably one of the best witnesses the Justice Department has ever had.

"We gave him a new identity and moved Tony and Flo to a small midwestern town. In fact, we moved them several times because they could not stay away from their children and some of their other relatives. He loved his children and later his grandchildren. He and Flo would phone them and arrange to meet them, and each time they risked discovery. They were also accustomed to a flashier lifestyle than the government provided and had always lived in big cities. Tony hated managing a shoe store, but there was a contract out on him, and he had little choice.

"A Mafia member swears an oath called the Omerta when he officially becomes a 'made member' of the family. The Omerta is essentially a vow to keep your mouth shut. Anyone who breaks the oath, and especially someone who cooperates with the government and testifies against other mobsters, is marked for death. It may take the mob years to find a guy, but they don't give up. The Mafia put a contract out on Tony, and for many years, for the most part, Tony behaved himself and hid behind his varied identities. He became a model citizen, even joined some civic groups. Flo was active in the PTA when the kids were growing up."

Addison got up and went to the table to pour himself a glass of water. He took a drink and then twisted the glass in his hands. The light from the desk lamp shone in his face, and Eve could see dark shadows under his eyes.

"Of course, what I'm telling you is not to leave this room, at least not for now," he said.

"Of course," Engstrum said.

"I was Tony's most recent contact. About six months ago, Tony got in touch with me and said he was leaving the program. He said he could no longer tolerate the constraints and limitations it placed on him and his family. He said he was willing to keep his latest identity—as I said, we had already changed it several times before because of lapses by either Tony or Flo—but he was going to move to a larger city, take trips, and live like a normal person.

"Of course, I tried to talk him out of it. I reminded him the contract on his life was still out there; in fact, it had been increased to five million dollars, the highest I know of for a Mafia hit. It shows how important he was to us as well as to the people who wanted him dead. I told him he was endangering Flo and their children, both of whom are married and have their own kids. But he wouldn't listen, and I personally think Flo, who never quite grasped the danger they were in, pushed him into the decision. She had never been happy in hiding. She wanted to see her family and play grandmother to her grandchildren. I guess you couldn't blame her for that. Despite her extravagances, some of them at government expense, she was a warm-hearted person."

Addison rose and started pacing the floor.

"I talked him into keeping the alias and told him to keep a low profile. I told him not to move to Chicago because he had too many old acquaintances who knew him there. But he insisted it would either have to be Chicago or New York. His daughter was in Chicago and his son in New York. He and Flo wanted to be near one or the other. It always seemed an inconsistency to me for a man who wouldn't blink an eye at killing someone to be such a strong family man," Addison said. "But Tony was." No one spoke when he paused as if to reflect on his last statement.

"Anyway, he said if he died, he died. He said at least he planned to live a little first. When a person decides to leave the program, we can't make them stay. He agreed to keep in touch with me, and I notified Emory, who had been his FBI contact. Needless to say, both of us were very worried. Emory also met with him and tried to talk him out of leaving. We knew as soon as they made contact with their children, friends, or relatives that it would not be long before the mob would get word. Against our advice, they chose to live in a suburb of Chicago.

"I kept in touch with them. About two weeks ago, Tony told me they were going on this cruise. He said they had never been to the Caribbean, and Flo was really excited about going. I warned him against it, as I had warned him about leaving the program, but I couldn't stop him. And to tell you the truth, it seemed to me like he was having the time of his life.

"I called Emory to let him know. He was worried because he was picking up information from an informant that the mob knew Tony had left, and his enemies had stepped up their search for him. Emory said he had heard a hit was being planned, but he did not know where or when it might happen.

“I contacted Tony immediately and told him about the danger. I urged him to cancel the trip and to rejoin the witness protection program so we could keep him safe. Emory pleaded with him, but Tony was not about to listen. He didn’t want to disappoint Flo, and he didn’t want to start over again with a new identity. Besides, he told me, the Caribbean would probably be safer than Chicago. He said he would consider rejoining the program when they got back, pointing out that the mob might want to kill him, but there was no evidence that anyone knew where he was or what he looked like.

“I thought Tony was probably right about that and that he would be safe until he got back. But a few days before the start of the cruise, Emory called to say he had heard they had located Tony and the hit might actually be made in the Caribbean because it would be more difficult for US officials to investigate.

“I tried to contact Tony, but he and Flo had already taken off by car for a trip to Florida before catching a plane to Puerto Rico. I then contacted the cruise line and found out a few journalists were going on the cruise. I quickly put my cover story together, and you know the rest,” he said.

Engstrum shot Mike a glance. Mike returned the look with a sheepish expression. “I never checked the Canadian magazine or checked his story,” he replied to Engstrum’s unasked question. “I usually contact everybody at their places of employment to arrange their trips, but I didn’t have time when Addison called. I knew we had room and told him he could join us in Saint Lucia as long as he could arrange his own airfare.”

“We’ll discuss it later,” Engstrum said, anger showing in his voice.

“You’re the only one who spotted me as a phony,” Addison said, looking at Eve. “How did you know?”

Eve’s eyes had not left his face during his narration. Now she studied her hands before she spoke. “You just didn’t seem like a journalist, especially a Canadian journalist. Your accent was wrong. Then you were very unfriendly, and most journalists are just the opposite."

"I didn't have much time to prepare," Addison replied dryly.

"What about Emory?" Engstrum asked. "He obviously joined you to help protect Tony, but what happened to him?"

Addison shook his head. "I don't know. I know he would never have left the ship, at least not voluntarily. He was a top agent, one of the best I've ever known."

"Then you think he may also be dead," Engstrum said.

"I don't know, but I can't think of any other plausible explanation for his disappearance," Addison replied, shaking his head. "He would never have gone anywhere without letting me know."

"Five million would be quite an incentive," Engstrum said.

"Never," Addison responded vehemently. "He had grown to like Tony and Flo. He would have given his life to protect them."

No one said anything. It was taking longer for their tired minds to respond. And no one liked the idea of another dead body on the ship and a killer on the loose.

"What was Tony's real name?" Eve asked finally.

"Anthony Antonelli," Addison replied.

Eve remembered reading about Anthony Antonelli in the newspapers. She had also seen his picture, but the Tony she had met when she boarded the ship bore little resemblance to the man in the photographs. Of course he was older, but this Tony was thinner, and his nose and mouth were different. It was amazing what plastic surgery could do. His changed appearance and status as a protected witness also explained why he did not want to be in the family photographs.

"He looked nothing like the newspaper shots I had seen of him," she said.

"Our surgeons do good work," Addison said.

"How did the assassin know who he was or where to find him?" Mike asked.

"We can only guess that they found out through Tony and Flo's contact with their family. They may have tapped their children's phones. Who knows? They knew Flo couldn't stay away from those grandchildren," Addison said ruefully. "They wanted Tony in the worst way. When he started talking, it really hurt their organization. It cost them both money and prestige. Letting him live would set a bad example."

Eve found herself thinking of Flo, the probable innocent in all of this, dead because she had remained loyal to the man she had married and the father of her children. She felt contrite for having thought ill of Flo's shopping sprees. Flo had told her the clothing stacked on the counter in Bequia was for her family, but Eve had doubted her. Now she knew she had misjudged her. Somehow knowing it made her feel worse about Flo's death.

"If they were after Tony, why kill Flo?" Engstrum queried. It was a good question and brought Eve's thoughts back to the present.

"I think the killer thought he had plenty of time to complete the contract," Addison said. "Most professionals are methodical and take time to plan a murder so they have the best chance of not being discovered and of setting up an escape route. In this case, he may have been enjoying the cruise while setting up his mark," Addison said.

The captain winced visibly at Addison's last remark but said nothing.

"I'm not sure the killer knew about me, but he may have recognized Emory because he had appeared as a witness at several of the trials. The mob knew he was the one who had gotten Tony to turn. Though the mob seldom kills FBI agents, killing Emory would probably earn the assassin a bonus," Addison said bitterly. "When he came aboard in Bequia, I'm sure it put a crimp in the killer's plans. He may have feared he would be recognized. Things had to be speeded up in order for the killer to avoid discovery. As for Flo, I suspect she just got in the way. Professional hit men don't like to leave witnesses who can identify them. All of this is speculation, and we won't know anything for sure until we find out what happened to Emory."

"Why choose my cabin?" Eve asked.

"I don't know," Addison said. "Maybe it was the closest one to where they were when he caught up with them. And maybe the hit man thought you might have had something to do with the FBI or police because you're always asking questions. Perhaps it was a warning to you," Addison said.

Eve felt heat suffuse her cheeks at the thought. Perhaps that was why Addison, the former abrasive Addison, had told her that her curiosity could get her into trouble. She would have to ask him, but now was not the time.

It was nearly four in the morning, and the only sleep she had had in two days was the brief nap on the beach. She was not sure how much longer she would last. Two dead people were in the shower in her cabin, and now Addison was telling her that she could very well be on a hit man's to-do list. She corrected herself to think "hit person" because no one knew the gender of the killer, though everyone was assuming it had to be a man.

"Did you search their cabin a few minutes ago?" Eve asked.

"I was going to, but I haven't had time," Addison said.

"It seems someone beat you—or us—to it," Engstrum said. He told Addison about the missing money.

"We suspected Tony had amassed a small fortune during his years as a criminal and had hidden it away, but I doubt that the money had anything to do with the hit unless the killer wanted to make it look like robbery was the motive," Addison said.

Engstrum cleared his throat. "We won't find out standing here. We have several problems that need to be addressed," he said. "We are currently cut off from the world because someone, I suppose the same person who killed the Maso—I mean the Antonellis—wrecked our radio and destroyed our other means of communication. Even if someone held on to their cell phone when they were supposed to turn them in, it is impossible to get a signal out here. We are in a dead zone.

"I could sail into port somewhere, but Mike has pointed out that if I do that, I'll be involving the local authorities in the investigation, and we could be held here for days or even weeks. That could be a problem for the passengers, not to mention the line," Engstrum said. "On the other hand, if I keep sailing around with a killer on board, I might be endangering the other passengers. My crew is unarmed. Your gun is the only one on the ship, except for the killer's. I don't feel safe, and the passengers will be ready to go over the side when they learn what has happened. We also need to do something with the bodies. They can't be left where they are. An autopsy needs to be performed, the crime scene examined, fingerprints taken, and whatever else is usually done…" Engstrum's voice trailed off.

"Is there a doctor on board?" Addison asked. "I can help with some of the crime work. I was a police detective before I joined the marshal's office. But I need someone with medical expertise to examine the bodies."

Mike and Eve looked at each other. "There's only Dr. White," Eve said. "He's the only one with medical training on board besides the nurses."

"He's a dentist," Addison said.

"He's all we've got," Eve replied.

"Then he'll have to do. I hope he's sobered up and still remembers enough of what he learned in basic anatomy to be of use."

"We also need to get a look at the passenger list to find out as much as we can about who is on board," Eve said. "It's going to be hard to check up on the passengers without a phone or radio."

"The lists are gone. Emory had already gotten them and had begun going over them. They were in his room, but they're gone now. I looked. I assume they may be at the bottom of the sea."

Engstrum looked startled. "How in hell did he get the lists? None of my crew gave them to him."

"I'm afraid there was no time to dwell on formalities. I believe he took them," Addison explained. "I suspect the killer probably took them when he took care of Emory."

"You should have told me what was going on," Engstrum said. "You had no right—"

"You're probably right, but we had no time to go through normal channels, and we were not authorized to tell anyone why we were here," Addison interrupted. "Our job was to try to get Tony and Flo off the ship and to safety. After that, we would have started looking for the hit man."

Mike walked to the door. "All may not be lost; I may have another list in my cabin. I usually like to keep one just to make sure I get everyone's name right. I'll see if it's still there."

"Let's hope," Engstrum replied. "If it's not, it would seem I'll have little choice but to get close enough to shore to send for the local authorities."

CHAPTER TWELVE

Dr. White had stayed up late playing cards and drinking rum. At home he preferred martinis, but the island rum seemed to be the right drink for the heat. This was his fourth *Sun Clipper* cruise. When his wife, Margaret, had been alive, they had gone on fancy cruises with their friends. They had dressed for dinner and danced the night away afterward. Dr. White had not particularly enjoyed the cruises. He had found them stuffy and too formal to be relaxing. He found himself thinking, if he had wanted to dress up every day, he might as well have stayed at home. At least it wasn't as hot in California. But his wife had loved the elegance, the fine food, nightly entertainment, and "putting on the dog," as White called it. He had not complained and had gone along with her wishes because after nearly forty years of marriage, he still loved her and wanted to please her.

But five years ago, Margaret had found out that she had breast cancer. Dr. White suspected she had known for some time about the lump in her breast, but she had said nothing to him. She had not gone to see a doctor or had an examination until she developed a cough in the winter that would not go away. By the time he forced her to see one of his colleagues, the cancer had spread to her lungs and other organs. She died six months later. He had felt as if he had failed her in some way, a way that had prevented her from confiding in him about the lump.

After her death, he found himself devoting hours to analyzing and remembering their years together, but even after reliving their marriage from beginning to end, for he had a very good memory, he still did not know exactly what he had done wrong. However, one thing that had struck him like a bolt of lightning was the knowledge that he had not made Margaret very happy, and he had failed to see her unhappiness. He had been too busy with his career to notice, and she had hidden it from him like she had hidden the lump. She had never let him down and had continued to play the role of the perfect wife, waiting and doting on him right up until the cancer made her too weak to get out of bed. Then she had died. After her death, he had begun drinking more than he should, but the alcohol did nothing to help him forget what he perceived to have been his shortcomings where Margaret was concerned. He concluded during his nightly stupors that he had been too selfish and busy with his own life to realize he was making the woman he loved miserable. It pained him to know that she had never really known how much he loved her. He had never told her.

The year following Margaret's death, 'he had agreed to take another cruise at his daughter Nancy's urging. But this time, he decided to try a barefoot cruise. He had run into people from these cruises on his more formal vacations with Margaret, and they always seemed to be having such a good time. Some of his previous cruise ships had been "fired on" and bombarded with water balloons lobbed onto their decks by passengers on barefoot cruises. Though Margaret had been shocked by the behavior, he had secretly envied the people whooping it up and lobbing the balloons. It looked like such fun. So he had booked his first passage with the *Sun Clipper* line and had returned for two weeks each year. He liked the drinking, the card-playing, hoisting the sails, and especially the horseplay. He liked not having to dress for dinner and being able to smoke his cigars without having to sneak off to a hidden place on deck. He liked walking around barefoot all day. Sometimes he fished off the deck with members of the crew, and they cooked his catch for dinner. There were no schedules to keep. If he wanted to go ashore, he did. If he wanted to stay on the ship and miss the island excursions, no one pressured him to do anything else. That was the key to his enjoyment. There was no pressure to do anything he didn't want to do. This was a real vacation. This was the life.

So he was not pleased when he heard someone knocking on his door at 4:00 a.m. He had stayed up late playing cards and drinking the night before and had planned to sleep late. After stumbling to the door in his undershorts and opening it a crack, White was even more annoyed when Vincent told him the captain needed to see him immediately.

"Can't this wait until morning?" White asked irritably. "If he has a toothache, tell him to take something for it."

"It's nothing like that," Vincent said, not giving any ground as White attempted to close the door.

White was not pleased. He had already been awakened earlier by some idiot crewman with a message for Emory. What would he be doing with Emory? he had asked the stupid man. He barely knew Emory. He was definitely going to complain about these interruptions, he thought as he glared at the crewman standing in the corridor. White's blood pressure rose another notch after he told Vincent he was going to go back to bed, but Vincent shook his head and refused to leave. White finally gave up and pulled on a T-shirt and shorts. He was still grumbling and making noises about filing a complaint or even suing the line when he reached Engstrum's cabin.

"What the hell's so damned important it can't wait until morning?" he demanded.

"We need your help," Engstrum said, making no attempt to apologize to White for disturbing him. "There's been a death—two, really. You're the only doctor."

"I'm a dentist," White said, turning to leave. "It was probably the food."

His exit was blocked by Addison, who stepped in front of him. "Maybe I should explain. Dr. White, the two dead people were murdered. You are the only doctor here. We need to move the bodies to storage, but we need someone to examine them first."

"Murdered? Did you say 'murdered'?" White blustered, his rum-reddened eyes widening in surprise.

"That's right," Addison said, pausing to let what he said sink in.

"Who are they? What happened? And while we're at it, who are you? You're that reporter who joined the cruise late," White said, pointing a liver-spotted finger at Addison.

Once more a flicker of a smile crossed Addison's face. "I'm Jerry Addison. I'm with the federal marshal's office. I can fill you in on the details while you're examining the bodies. We need to get started as soon as possible."

White had not moved. Now, he turned toward the captain, who nodded his head to verify what Addison had said. "You know the people as the Masons," Engstrum said. "They're both quite dead and appear to have been shot. We really do need your help."

White closed his mouth with a snap. "I'm a dentist," he said again. "You need a pathologist."

"You really are all we have," Engstrum assured him.

White was still mumbling half to himself that he was a dentist when the group reached Eve's cabin. Nothing White had seen in his early anatomy classes had prepared him for what he saw or smelled when he opened the door and stepped inside. His first reaction was to become sick. Then he chastised himself under his breath for having drunk too much.

"Take your time," Addison said. "Mike needs to get pictures before we move anything." White stepped back out into the corridor and drew in deep breaths of air, trying to overcome the nausea he was experiencing. His normally chubby red cheeks were suddenly deathly pale.

Mike moved around the cabin with his camera like a pro, following Addison's directions and snapping pictures from every angle. After a few minutes, he stopped shooting and looked inquiringly at Addison.

"That should do it for now," Addison said. "Now we need Dr. White."

Eve had remained outside the cabin to stay out of the way. It was crowded with only one person in it, let alone a group. She watched as White appeared to draw on some inner strength and force himself to go back through the cabin door.

"I'm a dentist," he muttered as he disappeared into the tiny room.

Eve watched from the door as White deftly examined the bodies. It was obvious that although he may have come across as something of a buffoon, he had not completely forgotten his early medical training.

After about twenty minutes, White, who had been making notes on a pad Mike had given him, announced that it would be all right to move the bodies. He had turned them over to examine the entry and exit wounds. He had ordered that their hands be wrapped in plastic bags scrounged from the ship's kitchen. Flo had not died quietly. She had fought with her assailant because White found skin beneath her fingernails and several of her long, red nails had been broken. That fact would make it easier to identify the killer if he had not found a way to get off the ship, Eve thought. The scratches would be fresh and should be easily visible. The skin could be matched in a laboratory.

Engstrum had ordered Vincent to have the cook clean out one of the ship's food lockers. He, Mike, and Vincent had fashioned body bags out of large pieces of plastic usually used to cover equipment. The bodies were carefully carried to the storage area off the galley and placed in the food locker, which Engstrum padlocked.

After the bodies were removed, Addison and Eve went over the cabin, carefully looking for anything that might not have been there before the murders. For Eve, it was easy to tell what was hers and what wasn't because she had so few belongings. All she had were a few toiletry items, the clothes she had bought at the ship's store, and the clothes she had worn the day she arrived.

Nothing unusual caught their attention. They were about to leave the room when Eve spotted something white that appeared to be a piece of lint sticking out from under her bunk bed. Upon closer examination, she found it was a piece of white cotton material attached to a small white button.

"Did you find something?" Addison asked.

"Just a button someone lost, unless Flo pulled it off in her struggle," Eve said, showing him the button. "Looks like it might have come off a shirt or blouse." The button wasn't off what either Tony or Flo had been wearing. Tony's white T-shirt had no buttons, and the buttons on Flo's blouse and shorts were gold.

Addison stuck it into a plastic baggie he had gotten from the kitchen and marked on a label where the button had been found. "It's such a common button, it probably won't be that much help. It could have been lying here for weeks. Even if it did come from the killer's clothing, the guy's an expert; he wouldn't keep a bloody shirt with a missing button," he said.

"Maybe he hasn't noticed it's missing, and there's no reason to believe the shirt has a lot of blood on it or any blood on it unless Flo scratched him enough to draw his own blood," Eve reasoned. "He obviously shot them after he got them into the shower. I doubt if he got in with them. He would have left bloody footprints, and there are none on the carpet. If he shot them somewhere else and dragged them into the shower, there would be blood elsewhere in the cabin and in the corridor. Everything had to have happened here, but the thing that's really bothering me is if Flo struggled with him, I wonder why no one heard anything."

Eve looked around the tiny cubicle again. It was so small and so close to the cabin next to it. Flo's thrashing should have been loud enough to alert someone. It only confirmed her previous assumption.

"I am reasonably sure it must have happened while we were all on deck firing the cannons," Eve told Addison. "The cannon fire would have covered the sound."

"That's a good possibility. But we won't know for sure unless Dr. White remembers enough of his training to establish a time of death. We really need a trained pathologist to conduct the autopsy and a forensic expert to go over this room properly," Addison said and sighed.

He and Eve had tried to touch as few surfaces as possible in their search just in case the killer had left fingerprints. Such normally routine investigative activities as dusting for prints, vacuuming for fibers and hairs, and collecting blood samples would have to wait until they could find an expert to examine the murder scene. Until then, they closed the cabin door and left another crewman whom Vincent had roused from his sleep to guard it.

They proceeded back down the corridor and up the stairs to Engstrum's cabin where White and the others had gone. Eve wondered what the point was in guarding the room instead of simply trying to lock it from the outside with a padlock. Perhaps Engstrum was buying the old cliché that a killer always returns to the scene of his crime, something Eve doubted a professional hit man would ever do. Eve suspected the killer was not plotting ways to get back into the room but ways to put as much distance as possible between himself and the killings. Chances are most of his time was being devoted to devising a plan to get off the ship, if he hadn't already gotten away. Of course, if he just waited long enough, the ship would eventually dock somewhere, and he would be able to leave with the rest of the passengers.

At Engstrum's cabin, they found White to be much more in control of his emotions than before. He was no longer mumbling to himself about being a dentist. Instead, he was rapidly writing notes on a large legal pad so he would forget nothing he had seen. He looked up when Eve and Addison came in and began speaking animatedly, a note of authority in his voice that had not been there before. He appeared to be pleased that he had been able to rise to the occasion.

"I would say you're probably right about the time of death judging by the temperature and humidity in the room and the current state of rigor mortis. I would say they were shot about the time we were all on deck firing those cannons," White said, looking at Eve. "We'll know more once an autopsy is performed and the contents of their stomachs are examined. Also, they were killed in the shower—probably led there and forced to get inside. I would say Tony was shot first, probably told to get into the shower first. Judging by the size of the wounds, the killer was about four feet away when he fired the first shot into his chest and much closer when he fired a second shot into his head. I would guess that Flo started to struggle with the killer after he shot Tony. She was shot at very close range in the chest and, I would guess, pushed backward into the shower as she fell. There are marks on the backs of her ankles where they hit the edge of the shower as she fell backward. She then apparently tried to crawl out of the shower but never made it. The head shots were fired at close range and at a downward angle, I suspect, after both were already dead or close to it."

"The kill shots," Addison murmured.

"Yes," White said, "quite right, the coup de grace. And probably with a smaller-caliber weapon, since the bullets are still in the bodies. We'll know more when we get them out."

After a silence of a few moments when everyone seemed to be digesting what White had said, Eve asked, "How much damage do you think Flo inflicted on the killer before she died?"

"A few scratches, probably not much more. A forensic pathologist could tell you more. And an expert on blood and spatter would certainly be a help here. Probably most of the blood belongs to Flo and Tony, but if she drew blood when she scratched her assailant, it would make identifying him so much easier with DNA testing and everything else available these days. I'm sorry I can't be of more help, but I'm a dentist," he added, some of his earlier confidence abandoning him.

Eve patted him on the shoulder. "You've done an excellent job. And when we get to civilization, the information you've collected will be invaluable," she said.

"We all appreciate what you've done," Engstrum added. "Now I would suggest we all try to get some rest. I've told Vincent to get some of the other crewmen up and to post guards at points around the ship, including the corridor outside your cabin. I plan to get the passengers together at ten o'clock to let them know what's happened and what we're doing about it. I wish I didn't have to say anything, but word travels quickly around a ship, and I want to prevent panic.

"I've also decided to sail for Green Parrot Cay. We can anchor out in the harbor to make sure no one leaves the ship until we're ready. We will be able to call the States and the authorities in Saint Vincent, who have legal jurisdiction on many of the islands in this region."

Mike looked about to open his mouth in protest, but Engstrum shot him a glance. "We'll try to do what we can without involving the locals, but I can't risk the safety of the passengers. I don't even have a gun or any kind of weapon. I got rid of my gun when I left the military. I never wanted to kill again," Engstrum said with uncharacteristic petulance. "We're sitting ducks if the killer strikes again. Meanwhile, without a means of communication and with some of our navigational equipment knocked out, we've had to come to a near standstill to avoid running into a reef. We'll travel in the daylight."

When Engstrum finished, he seemed weary and drained of energy. Eve too found the thought of bed suddenly appealing. Adrenaline had kept her going, but she could feel herself swaying. "I'll get you up before ten," Engstrum promised.

Addison caught her arm. "You can't go back to your cabin, but you can have the bottom bunk in mine. I prefer the top, anyway."

She didn't protest as he led her to his cabin and helped her into bed. She fell asleep before she heard him climb into the top bunk. As sleep overtook her, several thoughts crossed her mind in rapid succession. What if Addison was a phony? He had posed as a journalist; he could just as easily pose as a federal agent. What if he were the assassin? He had a gun, and he knew how to use it. He also had the cabin next to hers, and with the radio dead, there was no way to find out who he was.

The thoughts probably would have kept her awake if she hadn't been too tired to care.

CHAPTER THIRTEEN

Eve felt as if she were drifting somewhere off in space. In the distance, she could hear a rhythmic pounding and voices. But she resisted returning to the place where she had been before. Twice she had awakened, shaking in fear, her body drenched in sweat despite the ship's air conditioning. She had been dreaming, and in the dream Flo had been smiling at her, seemingly oblivious to the blood dripping from a wound in her ample chest as she heaped T-shirts covered with painted fish and birds on the counter in Melinda's store. Eve ignored the noise and willed herself to remain asleep. She wanted to continue drifting and to forget the terrors that had haunted her sleep. But the pounding and voices grew louder. And a moment later, she felt someone shaking her shoulder.

"Miss, you get up," Vincent said in his island accent. "The captain want everyone on deck. Sorry, I had to come in, but I worry when you don' answer." Eve could see the concern in his eyes. "I leave you now, but you don' get up; I come back," he said, closing the door behind him.

Eve pushed the sheet back and got up. It was a moment before she remembered that she was in Addison's cabin and not her own. She saw that his bed had not been slept in, and she wondered when he had left and where he had been while she slept. At least he had not killed her in her sleep.

She was still dressed in her *Sun Clipper* billboard outfit from the night before, but she had no intention of retrieving her other clothes from her cabin. She would buy more if she had to. Someone had brought her toiletry items from her cabin and laid them on the shelf by the sink. She guessed the thoughtful person had probably been Vincent, or perhaps even Addison, who was turning into a real surprise.

She splashed water on her face and ran a comb through her hair. There was no time for makeup, a low priority for her at any time. She thought again of Flo, always perfectly coiffed and manicured, now wrapped like a piece of meat and lying dead in a food locker. She shivered. Flo's death bothered her more than Tony's. He had chosen a lifestyle that often ended violently, but Flo was simply a wife, mother, grandmother, and compulsive shopper. Now she was dead because of a bad choice. She had married the wrong man.

Most of the passengers were already on deck when Eve arrived, but she saw no sign of Addison, Vincent, Charles, or the other crewmen who had been on guard the night before. Perhaps they were still guarding the lower corridors or had gone to bed. Eve suspected rumors of what had happened had already begun circulating because many of the passengers stood in groups, whispering to one another and looking pensive. Some were talking to Mike, who looked very tired and much older than he had the day before. Eve wondered if he had slept at all.

The Overtons hurried over to her, the looks of concern on their faces barely visible beneath the huge straw hats they wore. "Do you know what's happened?" Oliver Overton asked. "We've been hearing some terrible rumors about dead bodies. The Masons. The talk was all over the dining room at breakfast, but no one would tell us any details."

Though she said nothing, Eve could feel Cecilia Overton's eyes boring into her, demanding an answer. She wondered why she found them such disagreeable people, the kind who grated on her nerves.

"What makes you think I know anything?" Eve asked cautiously.

Both Overtons looked at one another and then said, "One of the nurses said you found them and that it happened in your cabin. We heard they were shot in your shower."

"Which nurse?" Eve asked, her anger at the ship's surprisingly efficient grapevine overshadowed by her interest in knowing how anyone not involved in last night's activities would have already found out about the murders.

"I think it's the one called Candy," Oliver said, looking at his wife for an assurance that he had not mixed them up. Both continued to watch her face, waiting for confirmation of the terrible deeds.

Damn Mike, Eve thought. He's been sleeping with Candy, and he probably told her. And she probably told the other nurses and, God knows, how many passengers they told about the two dead bodies in my cabin. If she had planned on doing a little detection before the passengers found out most of the details, the opportunity had already passed, thanks to Mike.

"I guess the captain will fill everyone in on what they don't already know," Eve said, thinking it wasn't much.

The Overtons looked disappointed. "We had hoped..." Cecilia began, her voice trailing off as she spotted Engstrum coming up the stairs from below deck. Without saying anything further, both turned and followed Engstrum to where he took a position in the middle of the deck.

Eve looked around and still saw no sign of Addison. She found herself beginning to worry about him.

Engstrum had begun speaking. First, he cautioned them not to panic at what he was about to tell them. "Bear in mind before I begin that everything is being done to ensure your safety."

Eve thought his words sounded hollow and not entirely truthful. How could he protect them? No one knew from whom they needed protection.

"Judging by the questions I've already been asked this morning, I guess some of you have already heard that the Masons are dead," he said, shooting a glance toward Mike, who was looking the other way. Eve decided that Engstrum was a rather observant fellow who had not taken long to trace the source of the leak. She also noticed, although the passengers murmured to one another and appeared quite frightened, that none seemed surprised at the news.

"We are doing what we can to look into the matter. We will be involving the local authorities when we determine jurisdiction. For the moment, we plan to head to Green Parrot Cay and to remain near the island until some of these decisions have been made," he said. "I know you are all anxious to leave the ship and to get on with your vacations, but I am afraid no one will be allowed to leave for the time being. I will ask that you remain on deck now because we are currently conducting a search of the rest of the ship. The search will include all the cabins." Engstrum paused and then continued. "And with your permission, of course, it will include a search of your personal belongings."

Several of the passengers began shouting questions at him, and a few objected to having their bags searched. He raised his hand for silence. Engstrum explained that passengers who wanted to be present when their cabins were searched would be called. "We'll try to inconvenience you as little as possible, but you must understand this is an unusual situation," he said.

That was the understatement of the year, Eve thought.

He raised his hand again for quiet. "Some of the crew are being posted at the stairs. If anyone needs to go down before we are finished with the deck below, a crew member will accompany you. The search of the dining area and the lower deck will be completed shortly so you will be able to return there. The cabin area below deck will take longer. I ask you to be patient."

Several passengers again spoke up, some wanting more details of the Masons' deaths and others wanting to know when they could leave the ship and how the captain planned to guarantee their safety.

"There are extenuating circumstances concerning the Masons' deaths," Engstrum said. "They involve things I cannot tell you at this time, but the circumstances make it unlikely that anyone else is in danger."

Eve wondered if Engstrum really believed what he had just said. As far as she knew, Emory had still not been found, and she had the distinct feeling that the killer was not particularly fond of her. Why else would he have chosen her cabin?

Harry Goldbaum, who Eve believed was one of several lawyers on the cruise, though she had not yet met him, asked the main question that was on everyone's mind. "How can you know we'll be safe if you don't know who killed them or why? Personally, my wife and I want to get off this ship as fast as possible. I think we all feel that way," Goldbaum said, looking at the other passengers. Most either nodded or voiced their agreement.

"I can assure you that your safety is uppermost in my mind. I have stationed crewmen on all decks to make sure you remain safe," Engstrum replied.

"What if one of them did it?" Goldbaum interrupted. "You really don't know what the hell you're doing, and you're putting all of us at risk. I say sail to the nearest port and let us all off."

Engstrum ignored him. "I have already launched an investigation. We are fortunate to have a member of a federal investigating agency on the ship. We will be conducting interviews to see if any of you witnessed anything."

Several passengers again began shouting questions, and another man, who reminded the captain that he also was a lawyer and whose name Eve did not know, informed Engstrum that he had no right to keep them on the ship.

"Would you rather be questioned by the authorities on one of the islands and possibly held as witnesses for days?" Engstrum asked. The idea had not occurred to most of the passengers and did not seem terribly appealing to anyone.

Goldbaum snorted. "That will eventually happen, anyway, won't it?"

"It's possible, but we are doing what we can to prevent it," Engstrum replied. Some of the fight and starch seemed to have gone out of him. He excused himself and went below.

A moment later, Vincent tapped Eve on the shoulder. "The captain and Mr. Addison want you," he said. "They need your help."

Eve followed Vincent, happy to have something to do to keep her busy and to get away from the furtive looks and questions from the other passengers. All of them knew it was Eve who had discovered the bodies. As she went below, she wondered what else could go wrong on this trip. She should have stayed in Cleveland, she thought. She might have been reporting on a murder, but at least she would not have been at the center of the investigation. Wait until Wally heard about this one. She almost missed him. She did not even want to contemplate the earful she would get from Irene.

When Eve opened the door to Engstrum's cabin, she found the captain and Mike leaning over the desk looking at a list of names. Mike waved it at her as she entered.

"At least he didn't get this one," he said. "Fortunately, I had it stuffed in one of my drawers and found it under my socks this morning."

Eve thought he seemed in good spirits for someone who had broken the captain's order to remain silent. Apparently, the harshest reprimand he had received was a dirty look. What ever happened to making insubordinate crew members walk the plank?

She would have gladly pushed him overboard herself for leaking information about the murders being committed in her cabin.

"You know," she began, looking at Mike, "your mouth has caused me all kinds of trouble. Don't you ever know when to shut up?"

Mike looked sheepish. "I'm sorry," he said.

"I've already spoken to him about it," Engstrum said. "But right now, we have more important things to be concerned with."

Eve looked at the list. She had seen most of the passengers on the list but could not put all of the faces together with the names. "What is it exactly that you want me to do?" she asked.

"I thought that with your investigative reporting skills, you might perhaps be able to determine who on this list is not who he says he is," Engstrum said.

"That will be a little difficult without a phone or communications of any kind," Eve said. She thought a moment. "Maybe we could at least eliminate some of the suspects by determining how many have been on prior cruises, if you know."

Engstrum and Mike both looked at each other. "That's good," Mike said. "I know some of these people from before. Take Dr. White. It's his fourth cruise."

"Probably his last after this," Eve quipped. Neither Mike nor Engstrum laughed.

"How do you know you can trust me?" Eve asked. "After all, the bodies were in my cabin."

Engstrum looked uncomfortable and eyed Mike.

"I know you are who you say you are because I called your office to talk to you while I was making your cruise arrangements," Mike said.

"Besides, I doubt you would have killed those people in your own cabin if you were the killer," Engstrum said. "Although this may sound chauvinistic, I don't think many women hire out for this kind of work."

"You mean to assassinate people?"

"Yes."

"Hit man wouldn't fit, would it?" Eve observed. "But the world is changing." Engstrum and Mike both smiled.

Engstrum left Mike and Eve to work on the list of names and went to see how the search was going. It was being conducted by Jerry Addison with the help of several members of the crew. So far, the searchers had not turned up anything of particular significance, and they still hadn't found Emory.

CHAPTER FOURTEEN

Addison was beginning to doubt the search would reveal anything. The weapon used in the shooting was probably at the bottom of the Caribbean, along with Emory's body. The thought that his long-time associate was probably dead was tough to take.

They were only about a third of the way through the cabins. The search was time-consuming because they had to go through everything, including the passengers' clothing, which, in some instances, was still in suitcases. And everyone had more than Eve, Addison thought wryly. He had instructed Charles and Vincent, who were working with him, to look for the murder weapon. They also were checking clothing for bloodstains or missing buttons. It was a long shot, but perhaps the killer might have overlooked the button when he changed clothes. Addison doubted it. The man was a pro and would have gotten rid of anything that would connect him to the crime. Now he was waiting for the ship to dock so he could walk down the gangway like any other tourist and go back to whatever rock he had climbed out from under without fear of arrest, Addison mused. But the killer had made one mistake, and that was letting Flo get close enough to scratch him.

He, White, and Engstrum had already surreptitiously checked over the passengers at breakfast for noticeable scratches. But the only one with a visible scratch was Mike, who had a large one on his neck next to a sucker bite. That was hardly a clue. Mike might have been a heartbreaker, but he doubted he was a mob hit man. Besides, he had been with the line for a long time. It wouldn't make sense unless he had been specifically recruited for the hit. Addison clung to the belief the killer was a pro and a first-timer on the *Clipper.* However, Mike or someone else who worked for the line would have been in excellent positions to place a hit man on the ship. It was an intriguing idea. The headquarters were in Miami and out of reach for now, but he could keep an eye on Mike.

Addison planned to take a turn on deck later to see who was being careful to keep covered. He had already entrusted White to keep watch until he got there. Again, Addison doubted they would get that lucky. For one thing, many of the passengers wore lightweight shirts most of the time unless they were swimming, and some even wore them in the water. Nowadays, everyone was afraid of getting skin cancer.

He felt certain that the only way they would find someone with scratches would be if the scratches were in a visible place, like the face, neck, or arms. Anything on the arms or torso might not be visible unless the killer had not yet noticed them himself and happened to remove his shirt. He doubted that Flo had grappled with the man's legs. By the time she was on the floor, she was near death. With that thought in mind, Addison concluded they were most likely to be on his upper body.

The investigation was not going to be easy. Even if they found someone with suspicious scratches, there would be no way to make a positive link without access to a laboratory. They had done what they could to preserve the bodies and the evidence under Flo's fingernails, but connecting the evidence with a suspect required forensic expertise. Holding someone without more evidence than a few scratches was going to be a tricky matter. He sighed as he dug into a suitcase the size of a steamer trunk.

An hour passed, and then two, without results. Engstrum had joined the search, and Eve had stopped by once to see how things were progressing. Each time Addison opened one of the showers, he found himself holding his breath, half expecting to find Emory's body.

At noon, Vincent stopped to inform the captain that the passengers were getting restless on the upper deck and wanted to know when they would be allowed into the dining room and the bar. A half hour later, after both Addison and Engstrum were sure every inch of the deck and the area surrounding the dining room had been searched, the captain gave the okay for them to return for lunch. The search continued below deck, and it was nearly three before a weary Addison called it off. They had found nothing of any significance in the cabins, engine room, kitchen, or crews' quarters. As he suspected, the killer had covered his tracks well.

No clue to Emory's whereabouts had been found either. The passengers were allowed to return to their cabins. Emory's, Eve's, and the one Tony and Flo had occupied remained sealed, and a crewman was posted in the corridor. On Engstrum's orders, crewmen also took turns standing guard in other parts of the ship to make sure the rest of the passengers remained safe.

As an added precaution, he suggested the passengers adopt a "buddy system" when they went below deck to their cabins so that none would be alone. No one missed the irony that Tony and Flo had been together when they were killed. However, those who were traveling together tended to stick more closely together, perhaps trusting only the ones who had come with them from home.

For much of the day, unbeknown to the passengers, Engstrum had set a rather rambling course in order to buy time so the search could continue unhampered by the involvement of any local authorities. He reasoned that if he reached Green Parrot Cay late in the day, he would have an excuse not to contact the police until the next day. The delay would give him time to phone Sinclair for instructions, and it would give Addison time to contact the FBI and the marshal's office.

Eve had suggested they might consider sailing back to Puerto Rico or even to Miami, but Engstrum knew the ship did not carry the supplies or fuel to make it without stopping. He had already made up his mind that if he got the word at Green Parrot Cay to go back without involving the local authorities, he would fuel up and stock up on food there.

Meanwhile, Addison and the captain had begun questioning the passengers in Engstrum's cabin. That went much faster than the search had gone. It seemed that no one had seen or heard anything out of the ordinary.

Mike and Eve were able to eliminate some of the passengers and crew from the list of suspects. Eighteen were on repeat cruises with the *Sun Clipper* line, and the odds of an assassin having taken a previous cruise seemed remote. They had also eliminated all but two crew members. Most had crewed on several trips or were known to Vincent who had been with the line since it opened.

That still left a number of potential suspects if you included some of the journalists. Mike wanted to take them off the list, which would have reduced the number by eight. But Eve was reluctant to remove the names of anyone she did not know until she could call the newspapers or magazines where they worked. She suspected Mike had not checked them out any better than he had Jerry Addison.

"Addison was a fluke," Mike fumed.

"No, he was a federal marshal," Eve snapped.

"Okay, but he was the only one I didn't have time to check because he joined the cruise so late. I'm sure I talked to all the others in their offices beforehand."

Though still not completely convinced of the thoroughness of Mike's background checks, Eve agreed to remove the writers from the list. The Overtons did not seem like killers to her. She knew she wasn't one, nor was Addison, unless he had fooled everyone and his badge was a fake. However, if that were the case, she would probably be dead instead of working on narrowing the list, no doubt killed in her sleep. She drew a line through his name. That left only an elderly couple from Arizona, who worked freelance for several newspapers and magazines, and a Florida couple Mike claimed to know personally. Eve wasn't sure she believed him, but she was too tired to argue.

Narrowing the list would have been a lot easier if she had access to a working phone, a computer, or a ship's radio. She had separated the list into men and women. Both she and Mike thought it was more likely that the killer was a man, though Eve was not ready to write off the women as suspects. But in her previous experience in covering the mob, she had found that most of their hired killers were men. It was a macho thing. Eve kept the women on a secondary list.

Tentatively eliminating the women from the primary suspect list further reduced the number of suspects to twelve. Eve pared the primary list by two more, removing Emory who could not be found and an elderly man who walked with a walker. Eve doubted he would have been physically capable of committing the crime unless he was faking his condition, which she doubted. She knew he would have been no match for Flo in a struggle.

By late afternoon, the primary list of suspects was down to ten. Addison and Engstrum were quite impressed when they stopped to check.

"Give me a phone, and see what I can do," she bragged, surprised by her own bravado. But without any means of communication, Eve decided her next plan of attack would be to get near the people left on the list. She would use her reporting skills to try to trap the phony. As it turned out, events on the ship continued to move so quickly that she was forced to suspend her interviews of the passengers until much later.

CHAPTER FIFTEEN

It was nearly dark when the ship anchored more than a half mile off the coast of Green Parrot Cay. Engstrum had chosen the spot and distance carefully, knowing even the strongest of swimmers would not chance a swim to shore from there because of the strong currents. The last thing he wanted was for the killer to slip into the water and get away.

He ordered the launch lowered. He had decided to take only Addison and Eve with him. Charles would drive. Despite his protests, Mike was told to remain on board to help members of the crew keep watch. Most of the passengers were on deck and anxious to get off the ship, and they watched enviously as the launch was lowered and the three passengers stepped into it. Charles started the engine, and they were off in a cloud of spray.

Eve felt refreshed as they pulled away from the ship and the wind blew through her hair, but her feelings of relief at leaving what had become a ship of doom in the vacation from hell was short lived. The launch had gone only a short distance when it began to take on water.

"Turn back!" Engstrum shouted to Charles. Charles tried unsuccessfully to turn the boat, which was rapidly filling with water and becoming as unwieldy as a bathtub. After a fruitless attempt to head back to the ship, the motor swamped and died.

While Charles tried to restart the engine, Engstrum frantically pulled up the seats and issued orders to get the life jackets that were normally stored under them. Eve, Addison, and Charles helped with the search, but the orange vests were gone. The flare gun for signaling emergencies was also gone. Though their futile search did not yield what they desperately needed, it revealed the cause of their problems. Holes had been carefully punched through the fiberglass on either side of the craft just above the waterline near the stern. The holes had not been immediately visible from the outside of the boat because the cutout pieces had been carefully taped in place so the boat would appear seaworthy. As long as the boat was empty, it floated. But once it was under way with several people in it, the stern sank into the water, and the bow rose enough for the water pressure to push open the holes, allowing the boat to take on water.

"The bastard," Engstrum muttered. "He's thought of everything, but how would he have known what we planned to do?"

Yes, how would he have known unless he were involved in the planning? Eve thought. She looked for something to hang onto that would float and remembered Mike's protests at being left behind. She wondered how genuine they had been.

But neither Eve nor anyone else had time to answer Engstrum's rhetorical question or to discuss how clever the killer had been in his efforts to keep anyone from getting to shore and a radio or telephone. Clearly, his goal was to force the ship to land so that everyone would disembark and he could slip away undetected, Eve thought as the water rose around her.

The boat was drifting rapidly away from the *Sun Clipper* and into a channel that would take them to the open sea. The chances of swimming back to the ship or the shore even for a strong swimmer like Eve were growing slimmer by the minute, and the chance of rescue from the ship seemed equally remote, since it was a good guess that the johnboat and the lifeboats had also been sabotaged. It was possible that those on board had not seen the launch go under. They had made it some distance from the ship before sinking, and it was already getting dark.

"Hang onto the boat! Someone will come to get us!" Engstrum yelled as the boat sank beneath the waves. Somehow his voice sounded less confident than his words.

"I had been wanting to go swimming all day," Eve said, trying to hide her fear as she struggled to hang on in the ever-increasing current, which threatened to tear the boat from her grasp. She could see that they were drifting toward the shipping channel. In the gathering darkness, it was altogether possible that they would be run over by a freighter or a cruise ship that would not see them, if they didn't drown first, she thought.

Meanwhile, the killer was probably back on the ship preparing to take over and sail to the nearest port. The passengers would probably help him. They wanted to get off the ship almost as much as the killer did. Engstrum had left the crew and Mike in charge, but Eve had decided that Mike was virtually worthless. Or was he? He was one of the few left on board who knew in advance of their plan to leave in the boat. He also knew which one they would be taking. Even though he had worked for the cruise line for some time, he could have been recruited for the hit. He had told her he was divorced with kids to support and was earning a lot less than he used to with the ad agency. He certainly could use five million dollars. Besides, his last name ended in a vowel, she thought, somewhat irrationally. So if Mike were the killer, that left Vincent in charge of the ship. He was trustworthy and kind but hardly a match for someone with a gun who had killed two people in cold blood, made an FBI agent disappear, and set four adrift to die in a leaky boat.

If she had only stayed home, Wally, her editor, would have been a happy man. Irene would not be worrying about her, and she would be with Keats, who missed her so much when she was away that he lost his feathers. Right now, she would have given anything to have been sitting in her apartment. She would have even tolerated Irene saying in that annoying voice she used when she wanted to rub it in, "I warned you, didn't I, dear? You'll believe me next time." Anything was better than clinging to the side of a submerged launch in the Caribbean, hoping not to die.

All she had wanted was a restful week in the Caribbean away from the pressures of work. A cruise had sounded so wonderful and peaceful. But after two days in what should have been paradise, she had had only a few hours' sleep, found two dead bodies in her shower, lost her luggage, and was probably about to drown or be run over by a freighter. So much for rest and relaxation. She wondered if she could sue. She doubted a jury would award much for pain and suffering incurred on a free cruise. If she lived, she would have better luck collecting from the airline for her lost luggage. If she didn't make it, she would not need her luggage.

But why was she even thinking about these things now? She should be concentrating on ways to survive…and what that was that had just brushed against her leg. It had to be a shark. She stifled a scream. She loved swimming and snorkeling, but she hated deep, black water.

"There's something in the water!" she yelled, trying not to sound altogether hysterical.

"Just a fish," Charles said, his voice rising over the sound of the surf.

"It brushed my leg."

"The sea is full of fish; most won't hurt you," he said, trying to calm her.

Addison, who was on the other side of the boat, worked his way around toward her.

"It's okay," he said, wrapping an arm around her to keep her from slipping off the boat. "Just hold on. It's better to stay with a sunken boat as long as part of it still floats than to risk a swim in the dark. With luck, we'll drift to shore."

"I'm a good swimmer," she protested. "I just prefer pools, at least at night when you can't see what's in the water with you. I don't want to be eaten," she said.

"I swim in the sea all the time," Charles said. "There is nothing to worry about. With luck we can drift to a reef and climb out."

"That's a good thought!" Engstrum yelled. "Let's try to turn the boat toward shore and kick in that direction. There are reefs near the end of the island, and maybe we can make it to one of them before we float past."

"It would be best to angle the boat so we are not fighting the current so much," Charles said.

They could barely make out the outline of the island in the dark, but they began to kick and paddle in its general direction. At least an hour passed, and they could no longer see the island or any lights. Eve was certain they had already floated past it and were drifting in the shipping lane. They stopped paddling because they were tired and seemed to be making little progress. It was hard to fight the current and move the submerged craft through the water.

Fatigue was plaguing all of them, and Eve wondered how long they would be able to hang onto the boat. She hadn't planned to die at sea, but she felt her own grip slipping, and she was getting very cold. At least nothing had bumped her leg for a while.

"Hang on," Addison said. "If you're too tired, we'll push you into the launch."

"I can hang on longer," Eve replied. Her arms ached, and her fingers were numb from gripping the side; she guessed the others were not feeling much better.

The tug of the current seemed to have slowed. They had undoubtedly drifted into the shipping lane without lights or any way to warn an approaching vessel of their presence. Most pleasure boaters tended to put to shore at dusk, but the larger ships, some fishing vessels, and, in these parts, drug smugglers often sailed these waters at night. Of the choices of types of ships to possibly cross their path, Eve hoped for a friendly island fisherman, who would take them aboard, offer them hot coffee, and agree to take them anywhere they wanted to go. She had just started daydreaming about where that might be when she heard the low rumbling of an engine in the distance. It was followed by two blasts of a ship's horn. Turning, she saw the ship outlined in the moonlight. It was as big as a mountain and bearing down on them at full speed.

Simultaneously, they began yelling in the unrealistic hope that someone on board would see them and steer away. But no matter how loudly they shouted and yelled, the boat continued toward them.

"Swim!" Engstrum and Addison yelled almost in unison. Eve let go of the boat and swam away from the oncoming ship with a renewed strength she had not known she possessed. Addison and Charles were next to her, stroking as hard as they could go. They had gone only a few yards when they heard the sickening sound of the large ship crushing what was left of the launch. A moment later, Eve was swamped in the ship's wake, and she struggled for breath as waves washed over her head.

She surfaced, coughing and sputtering but in one piece. She was unable to see anyone else and was afraid she was all alone. Then Addison surfaced next to her, and a moment later she spotted Charles's white teeth as he smiled in the darkness. The only one missing was Engstrum. He had gone in the opposite direction and did not answer their calls. They did not know if he had gotten out of the way of the ship fast enough to survive. Those aboard had not seen them or felt the impact of the collision, for it continued on its way without even slowing.

"I'll look for him," Charles said, when their yells failed to elicit a response. "You stay here."

"We'll come with you. We aren't going to make it unless we swim," Eve said. She had barely gotten the words out of her mouth when a piece of wood smacked the side of her head. It was the first time she could remember being pleased at almost being knocked senseless. She grabbed onto the wood, which remained afloat under her weight.

"I've got one of the seats!" she yelled. "It floats. Let's try to find a couple more. We can hang onto them and try to paddle toward shore, if we can decide where that is. We've got to find Engstrum and get out of the shipping lane."

Charles had already disappeared in his search for the captain; Eve and Addison were left alone. They managed to snag four wooden seats from the launch, enough for everyone, including Engstrum, if he were found. Holding onto the seats made movement through the water easier, and Eve found that swimming and treading water had raised her body temperature to a more comfortable level. Despite the near miss with the ship, she was beginning to get her second wind.

Several minutes went by before they heard Charles yelling, "I've got him!"

"Stay here," Addison said. "I'll be back."

"I'm not going anywhere," Eve replied.

Addison piled two extra boards on top of his and pushed off, paddling in the direction of Charles's voice. After a moment, he disappeared into the gentle swells and the darkness. She was all alone in the sea. This was definitely not in the brochure, she thought.

CHAPTER SIXTEEN

It seemed like hours had passed, but it was probably only a few minutes before Eve heard Addison calling her.

"We've got him, but he's hurt!" he yelled. "Are you still there?"

"I'm here!" she yelled back as loudly as she could.

After another few minutes, she saw three heads bobbing in the water and breathed a sigh of relief. If she were going to die, for some illogical reason, she did not want to die alone. As they drew nearer, she could see that Charles and Addison were holding Engstrum on one of the boards and pushing him through the water. He did not seem to be helping.

"He got hit in the head," Addison said. "He's out of it. It's a wonder he stayed afloat long enough for Charles to get to him." His voice was coming in breathless gasps.

Eve could see a gash in Engstrum's forehead, and he appeared to be unconscious. They pushed their boards together and treaded water furiously, but they all knew the only way they could possibly survive was to get to shore. The problem was determining where that was in the dark. Charles and Addison led the way, holding

Engstrum on the board and pushing him through the surf. Eve thought their chances of making it were not good, and she hoped they wouldn't be flattened by another ship before they got out of the shipping lane. Maybe they would be lucky enough to reach a coral reef and shallow water where they would be safe from larger ships and possibly find a place to stand until it got light. The sea was full of reefs.

She tried not to think about the trail of blood that Engstrum's head wound was leaving in the water or the dorsal fin she had spotted earlier. That was another reason to get to shore before they became shark bait. The thought of being stung by the fire coral that dotted the reefs was more appealing than being eaten. In black water you could not see what was swimming with you.

But even the sky was not cooperating. Unlike most starry nights in the tropics, the air had become heavy with an oncoming storm, and clouds obscured the stars and the moon. The gentle swells were turning to a heavy chop, which made it harder to stay afloat. All around the sea was dark and ominous. Eve wondered how much longer they could hang on. Engstrum was still unconscious and perhaps dying. They had no way to assess his condition and no medical equipment to help him. Once fatigue and cold set in, they would not be able to make it to shore. They did not know where land was, anyway, or if they were even going in the right direction. Now they could not rely on the stars to guide them.

If they did not get eaten by one of the sea's predators, they would surely drown. For the first time, she felt the beginning of despair.

It was some time later, when Charles stopped paddling and raised his head to listen. Eve did not think they had progressed very far, but she had heard a sound too. She tried to put it out of her mind, fearing she was hallucinating like people on the desert who see waterfalls. But the sound grew louder, and she recognized it to be the throbbing of a boat engine. It wasn't the kind of rumble that had signaled the approach of the large ship that had run them down. It sounded like the throb of the engine on a small boat. All three of them stopped paddling and listened. As if on cue, they began yelling and waving their arms. It was definitely a boat coming in their direction, and it was small enough that they had a chance of being seen or heard.

"If we only had something white to attract their attention!" Addison yelled. He looked at Eve's T-shirt. "Do you mind?"

This was no time for modesty, Eve thought, and pulled it over her head again, handing it to Addison, who looped it over his board and began waving it in the air and yelling at the top of his lungs. Moments later, it sounded as if the small boat had slowed and turned in their direction.

It was almost upon them before they saw it bobbing through the water and heard Vincent calling out. "I was afraid I'd never find you," he said as he brought the craft alongside them. He shut off the motor and pulled them into it one by one. Engstrum was laid flat and a cushion placed under his head. Vincent had brought blankets, which they wrapped around him. Eve shared one with Addison. She was shivering and wearing only a bra because her T-shirt was gone. She would have to buy another one. This trip had definitely been hard on clothes.

"We didn't think you saw us sink," Addison said.

"I saw you but could do nothing until I fixed the boat. Someone had poked holes in the side of it. I had to patch it before I could use it," he said.

"How did you spot the holes?" Eve asked.

"After you sank, I checked all the boats and found they had all been sabotaged," Vincent said. "This one had the least damage, so I fixed it."

"How did you find us?"

"I know the currents. I followed them hoping you would have drifted this way," he said, smiling, his even, white teeth gleamed in the darkness.

Engstrum began to stir and was regaining consciousness, but he moaned in pain. It was decided to take him back to the ship after Vincent explained that the island remained some distance away. He was also worried that the hastily applied boat patch might not hold up to the increasing waves.

Dr. White and the nurses would be able to care of Engstrum and stitch up the gash on his head. They would rest and try to reach the island in the morning when it was daylight.

Eve's spirits had begun to rise, although they no longer had the passenger list or her pared-down list of suspects, which had gone down with the boat. Eve had planned to begin checking the people on the list as soon as she had access to a phone or computer. Addison had planned to give it to the FBI, but now it was at the bottom of the sea. Eve hoped the duplicate list Mike had kept was still safe. If not, she could make another one from the list Sinclair probably kept at the main office, if she ever got to a phone. But any delay would give the killer more time to get away.

"Is everything okay on the ship?" Addison asked, once they were settled and under way.

"It was quiet when I left. The passengers were asleep," Vincent said. "But something bad did happen after you left." He hesitated, reluctant to be the messenger of more bad news.

"What was that?"

"We found Mr. Emory," Vincent said. "He was in one of the lifeboats."

"Dead?"

"Yes. It looked like he was shot too. Dr. White examined him like he did the others, and Mr. Mike took pictures. But we left him there until you got back so you could look. James is guarding the body," Vincent said matter-of-factly.

"We never looked in the lifeboats," Addison said. "We looked everywhere else but not in the boats." Eve thought Addison looked sadder than she had ever seen him.

"I'm sorry," she said, laying her hand on his arm.

"He was a friend. The best," Addison said. "I'm going to catch the bastard who did this." The anger he felt rang in his voice.

Eve had seen that kind of reaction before. She guessed it was what all police felt for a fallen comrade. While solving the murders of citizens was police business, avenging the murder of a comrade was personal. It was not unlike the loyalty felt among investigative reporters. She remembered when one was killed in a car bombing in Arizona a number of years ago, members of IRE (Investigative Reporters and Editors) descended on the area from around the country and had not only continued the slain reporter's investigation but also had brought his killers to justice.

The news of Emory's death hung over them, and no one said much for the rest of the trip. They were exhausted. Eve felt waterlogged, her throat was sore, and she was thirsty from swallowing salt water. Though it had seemed as if they had drifted miles from the ship, it wasn't long before they saw the lights of the *Sun Clipper* in the distance. Eve thought it looked more lit up than usual, and she found she was correct as they drew nearer.

Vincent explained that he had decided it would be safer to leave more deck lights on because they were anchored further out in the main channel than usual, and it would make it easier to see if anyone attempted to swim ashore. He had stationed crew members at locations throughout the ship and set up a rotation schedule so that some slept while the others remained on guard. He seemed to be an untiring marvel of organization and quiet authority. He would have made an excellent captain of his own ship, Eve thought. Perhaps the line would consider a promotion after this cruise. She would certainly put a word in for him. After all, he had just saved their lives.

They were helped on board by several members of the crew who were genuinely pleased to find out that they had survived. Charles seemed somewhat embarrassed by the hugs he received from fellow crewmen.

Vincent sent someone to awaken Dr. White and Candy to take care of the captain. White must have been sleeping in his clothes because he appeared almost immediately. He had Engstrum taken to his cabin where he could minister to him. Candy appeared bleary eyed but uncomplaining. Mike accompanied her, looking even more haggard than he had the day before.

"You look like hell," he said to Eve.

"So do you," she replied. Then he hugged her, startling the hell out of her.

"What's the matter with you?" Eve asked.

"I was afraid you were dead," Mike admitted, a grin lighting up his unshaven face.

"I'm fine. We're fine," Eve said. "Vincent found us just in time."

"I don't think I could have handled much more death this trip," Mike said. "I may find a new line of work when I get back, if I get back. My old job isn't looking as bad as I used to think."

"My job's looking pretty good right now too," Eve said. Her legs were rubbery, and she knew that if she did not get to bed within the next few minutes, she would collapse and sleep wherever she landed.

"You heard about Emory," Mike said, looking at Addison and Eve as he spoke.

They nodded. "I'd like to see him," Addison said. "Vincent said he hasn't been moved yet."

"We left him where we found him so you could get a look before we moved him to the locker." Mike led the way to the lifeboat where Emory's body had been found. The boat was usually hung above the deck, and Eve wondered how the killer had gotten Emory into it before killing him.

As if reading her mind, Mike said, "I think he must have lowered the boat and then raised it after he put Emory inside of it. That's the only way I can figure it."

"He'd have to be pretty strong to do that...unless he forced him to climb into it before he shot him," Addison said.

Eve found it hard to believe that Emory, a trained professional, would have allowed himself to be forced to climb into the boat before he was shot, but it was possible the killer had lured Emory into a trap. Maybe he had told him something that had made Emory want to look in the boat, and he had climbed up there himself. In any case, he had been dead for some time. The body was beginning to smell.

It lay stuffed under the seats in a pool of blood. Eve could see that blood was matted in Emory's hair, and there was a dark stain in the middle of his back. Emory appeared to have been shot in the back and once through the head. The method of death was similar to the way the others had been killed. After a brief examination, Addison instructed two crew members to wrap the body and take it to the food locker.

"If this keeps up, we'll need another locker," Mike said. Addison shot him a dark look, obviously unable to appreciate his weak attempt at gallows humor.

A few minutes later, Eve excused herself, planning to get some rest before it was time to get up again. It was already nearing morning. But as she descended the stairs to the lower deck, Vincent shot past her taking the steps two at a time.

"What's the matter?" she called after his retreating form.

"Someone's been in the locker. I'll get Mr. Jerry, and you better come too."

Addison joined her on the stairs, and they moved as quickly as their tired legs could carry them to the meat locker in the galley. The door stood open now, the hasp that held the padlock dangled from where it had been pried off. Eve watched in horror as Vincent reached inside and lifted one of Flo's lifeless arms. Her hand had been chopped off at the wrist. The same was true of her other hand. Eve was overcome by nausea just as she had been when she first found the bodies in her cabin. She rushed to the sink. No one paid attention to her. Addison was firing questions at Vincent who was translating for the frightened cook who spoke little English.

"The cook says the only time he left the galley last night until he went to bed was when Mr. Mike told him to take food to one of the passengers who wasn't feeling well. He says he was gone only about ten minutes," Vincent said.

After delivering the food, the cook had gone to bed. He had come in early this morning to begin getting breakfast started for the early risers and that was when he noticed that the padlock had been pried off the door and the locker opened. He found his chopping block and cleaver were dirtied and lying on the counter. "That was when he opened the locker and found the woman's hands had been chopped off," Vincent said. "I heard him yelling for help." The cook continued to tremble as he related the tale of his grisly discovery.

"Did Mr. Mike come himself, or did he send someone with the message?" Addison asked.

"Neither," Vincent said. "He sent a note. The cook said he found it on the counter when he came back from the bathroom. He thought nothing of it. He made some sandwiches and took them to the passenger's cabin, but no one was there. He waited a few minutes and then left them on the dresser.

By now, Mike had heard the commotion and joined the group in the galley. He was grim-faced when Addison confronted him about the note. "I never sent a note about any sandwiches," he said. "Let's see it. Let's see if it's my handwriting."

Addison turned to Vincent. "Ask him what he did with the note."

"The cook said he left it on the counter, but it's gone now."

Eve had regained control of her stomach and watched Mike's face. His denials seemed sincere, but it would be impossible to know whether he was telling the truth unless they found the note. She motioned to Vincent, and they searched the floor near the counter and finally went through the garbage but found nothing resembling a note. Eve had allowed Vincent to do most of the probing through the garbage, not wanting to grab ahold of a severed hand in the refuse.

"Well, that means the skin samples under her fingernails are gone," Eve said. "There's no way to get a match now. The hands are probably at the bottom of the sea. We don't have the note, and we are no nearer to catching the killer. The only thing we do know is that he is still quite active and still on the ship."

Addison studied Eve's face for a long time before he spoke again. "You're right," he said finally. They searched the kitchen again but found no sign of the note or Flo's hands. Addison bagged the cleaver and covered the chopping block, hoping that prints could be lifted later.

"Get some rest; you look ready to collapse, and there's nothing you can do here. I'm going to question the cook, though I doubt I will learn much from him." Turning to Mike, he said, "We'll talk afterward."

Eve needed no further encouragement to leave the galley. It was getting light outside, but she was too tired to stand, let alone to think. She found her way to the bottom bunk in Addison's room and fell into it. She slept so soundly that she never heard Addison come into the room.

He stood looking at her for several minutes before climbing into the top bunk and falling asleep.

CHAPTER SEVENTEEN

Eve and Addison sat up almost in unison. Sun was streaming in through the porthole next to the upper bunk, but it was not the sun that had awakened them. It was the noise coming from the upper deck. They could hear yelling, and within seconds a crewman pounded on the door.

"Come quick! Someone's in the water!" he yelled.

Eve grabbed her still-damp shorts and undergarments from where she had hung them on a hook.

"Could you loan me a T-shirt?" she asked, holding the sheet around her as she pulled her clothes on under it.

"Help yourself," Addison said, gesturing toward the chest of drawers as he headed out the door, pulling a shirt over his head as he ran.

Eve grabbed the first shirt she came to, noting that it too was a billboard for the *Sun Clipper.* She resigned herself to the fact that on this trip she would never escape looking like a cruise-line advertisement. At home she preferred plain, even passing up bargains in designer clothing that had the designer's name prominently displayed in such a way that it could not be removed.

This was not the time to be picky about her wardrobe. She raced up the corridor and bounded up the steps to the upper deck, surprised that her legs were able to move so quickly given their rubbery condition a few hours earlier. She was panting by the time she hit the top step. Passengers were leaning against the railing, watching and yelling to someone splashing around in the water below.

Several members of the crew had already lowered the boat Vincent had repaired, the only one that would still float, and were attempting to pull the swimmer from the water. This was proving to be a difficult task because the individual did not seem to be cooperating. It was too far away for Eve to recognize who it was, but she fervently hoped it would turn out to be their killer so they could all return to a reasonable degree of normalcy on the ship, at least as reasonable as could be expected following the murders of three people.

At this point, Eve had given up all thought of enjoying the vacation. Now she would settle for surviving it long enough to catch a plane home. So much for romantic Caribbean cruises. She would try the mountains next time.

She chose a spot along the railing next to Addison, who was intently watching what was transpiring below.

"That's Ulrika," Candy said, moving up beside them.

Eve recognized the plump Canadian nurse with the German accent.

"She's been completely freaked out since those people were found dead. I think finding that guy last night really put her over the edge. All she could talk about was getting off this boat before someone murdered her," Candy said. "She isn't even a very good swimmer. Look at her."

Eve met Addison's glance. She saw disappointment in his face.

"She would not have been strong enough to raise the lifeboat," he mumbled as he walked away, heading toward the lower deck where Ulrika would be brought up the ladder.

"Not unless she had help or he got into it himself," Eve said, turning to follow him.

"Why would he do something stupid like that?" he asked, striding toward the stairs. He was no longer listening.

She looked back toward the lifeboat that had contained Emory's body. It was once more raised above the floor of the deck, only this time it was covered with a tarp to preserve any evidence that might be found inside it by a forensic team, should they happen to find one hanging around one of the islands. A section of the deck below the boat had been roped off by the crew to keep the passengers away from the area, but the rope was having little effect other than to make some of the passengers bend over as they walked under it. So much for preserving evidence.

Ulrika was still struggling with the crew as they brought her up the ladder. "I have a right to leave. I'm not a prisoner on dis det ship," she said. She obviously meant to say "death" ship, but her accent was becoming more noticeable as she became more hysterical. "Vee are all going to be murdered!" she shrieked.

Addison told the crewmen to take her to an empty cabin where he could question her. Eve was about to follow, but he motioned her back.

"Stay here. This won't take long, and maybe you can pick up something useful by mingling with the other passengers."

Eve didn't mind not being included. She doubted Addison would learn much from Ulrika, and she was surprised to find she was starting to feel very hungry. She wandered into the dining room. It was way past breakfast time, but some of the passengers had lingered over their food, and she hoped she could still get something to eat. Even a greasy American breakfast of bacon and eggs was starting to appeal to her. She had not eaten since lunch the day before.

She chose a place at a table with the Overtons. As usual they were completely swathed in clothing, though there was hardly any danger of sunstroke in the dining room, Eve thought.

"I can't believe all that's happened," Cecilia began. "This is just terrible."

Eve was already regretting choosing their table. She was not in the mood to be grilled or to gossip about the murders.

"I heard you almost drowned last night," Cecilia began. "What happened?"

"The boat sank," Eve said simply, hoping the brief explanation would suffice but knowing it wouldn't.

"But why did it sink? And how did they ever find you?"

"You'll really have to ask Vincent. I'm too tired to talk about it right now," Eve said. She knew she was starting to sound crabby. It was a trait she had possessed since childhood. She got crabby when she was tired and when someone was bugging her.

Oliver said nothing throughout their exchange, but now he patted his wife on the arm.

"Eve has been through quite an ordeal, and I'm sure she'll tell us about it after she's rested."

Bless you, Eve thought.

Cecilia looked disappointed, but she did not ask any more questions. After sitting for a few more minutes in uncustomary silence, they said their good-byes and left.

"It's just lucky Vincent found you," Cecilia said as they walked away.

You're damn right, Eve thought.

Eve did not see anyone waiting on tables. Everyone had already eaten, though many of the tables had not been cleared. She supposed most of the crew who usually worked the dining room had been pressed into guard duty. It was looking like she wasn't going to get anything to eat, and the food left on some of the plates by other passengers was beginning to look appetizing. Eve was reaching for a stray piece of toast left on a bread plate when a crewman materialized at her side.

"Vincent said you might be hungry, miss. Can I get you anything?"

Vincent to the rescue again, Eve thought. Didn't he ever sleep? Eve smiled and tried to withdraw her hand from the plate as casually as possible.

"Yes, I am a little," she said. The crewman, whom Eve did not know by name, smiled.

"I'll be right back," he said.

Eve's food of scrambled eggs and bacon had just arrived, and she was scarfing it down like a person at a hunger station in Ethiopia when Addison plunked himself down beside her.

"She's not who vee vant," he said, imitating Ulrika's accent. "She's just terrified like most of the other passengers, but she's showing less restraint. They all want to get off this tub, and I can't say I blame them." The luxury yacht had now become a tub, Eve thought. It's amazing how quickly murder can take away the glamour.

"I'd like to be somewhere more pleasant myself," Addison said. "I don't know how much longer we can keep the rest of the passengers here, and if they all make a break for it, it will kind of defeat the purpose of keeping them isolated, won't it?"

Eve knew he was right. It was probably what the killer was waiting for too—for the passengers to force the ship to land so he could walk away. They'd never find him then. It would just be another successful Mafia hit, except, of course, for Emory. Why had he been killed? She didn't really think it was for revenge because he had testified against a member. The Mafia usually didn't kill members of law enforcement for doing their jobs.

"Did you come up with anything?" he asked hopefully.

"No," Eve replied. Now that she was full, she was regretting that she had wasted so much time stuffing herself. "Did you find out anything useful from the cook?"

"Only that the sandwiches went to a cabin shared by two guys, last names Ridge and Amsterdam. I'll question them, but you might try to find out something about them."

She told Addison about trying to question Ridge the night of the murders, about seeing the two men on the deserted beach in Bequia, and about the odd conversation she had overheard on deck. "I'm sure Ridge said something to the effect that it would all be over soon. I guess, in itself that wasn't particularly incriminating, but I would consider it suspicious."

Addison didn't recall seeing them on the beach when he and Emory had met with Tony in their effort to get him to leave the cruise and rejoin witness protection.

"Perhaps they followed you and stayed out of sight," Eve said. "Perhaps they overheard the conversation and stepped up their plans to kill him. Maybe two people were sent to do the job."

Addison shook his head. "Anything's possible. I don't know what to think, but their being on the beach sometime after we had been there doesn't mean a thing. I'm sure lots of people have discovered that beach and like it because it's more isolated. As for the conversation you overheard, I don't know what to make of what you overheard. It could mean anything, and it is worth checking out. I'll ask them about it."

Addison rose to leave.

"Okay, I'll find Mike and try to reconstruct that list, unless you think I should add his name to it after last night…or rather this morning," Eve said, correcting herself.

Addison shook his head. "I don't think so, but I really don't know."

"I'll leave him off for now, but I'll keep an eye on him," Eve said. "I do wish we could get to a phone. It would make this so much easier. Maybe we should try to get to shore again."

"I'm afraid that won't be possible now, at least not for a few hours. Vincent did the best he could to patch the hole in the boat, but it's taking on too much water now. It's lucky he was able to get to us and rescue Ulrika before the first patch let loose."

"Can he fix it?"

"He's trying."

"So we're stranded again."

"Afraid so," he said.

Eve did not like the prospect of being cut off from the world any more than the other passengers did. It would have been different if a killer with a gun were not somewhere on the ship. They would have to find him and hope that they could subdue him before he killed again. Adding to their vulnerability was the fact that Addison had lost his gun when the launch sank. The good guys were unarmed. Eve suspected the killer, on the other hand, had managed to hide his weapon in case he needed it. She doubted if he would be unarmed when they finally found him.

CHAPTER EIGHTEEN

They were in luck. Mike had kept a duplicate list of names in his cabin. He and Eve began poring over the names on her short list of suspects. She tried to identify the people but was not as familiar with them as Mike. She had only been on the ship for two days and had spent much of that time finding dead bodies and trying to survive a near-death experience. She paid less attention to the names than to the occupations, which she began to piece together based on what Mike knew from his conversations with them.

Eve had her own ideas about the assumed occupation of the person she was looking for. She doubted that a hit man would pose as a doctor or lawyer. People always asked them for free advice, and he might be spotted as a phony if he were unable to convincingly fake it. The only doctor was Dr. White, and he was a dentist who had taken many cruises. She was sure he was not the killer. There were several lawyers, but though she had little use for their breed in general, they had not made it to her short list. Most were traveling with their wives and had been on previous cruises.

The killer would be more apt to choose a job or profession that few passengers would ask questions about. If questions were asked, it would be the kind of work with which he was familiar and could easily provide responses. It might be one he had used before; in fact, if he were a pro, as Eve suspected, he might also have several identities, including a new one to disappear under once they docked.

She tried to put herself in his place, wondering what identity she would assume if she wanted to cover up who she really was. Maybe she would pose as someone in sales, like a manufacturer's rep or a small business owner. As a reporter living overseas, she had met a number of people whom she knew were connected with the CIA. Most had posed as diplomats working at local consulates or embassies. Some who were traveling through had pretended to be representatives of "research" companies gathering information on business or political trends. Others worked for front organizations or even as newspaper reporters, a choice she considered quite loathsome because of her pride in her profession.

Stateside, the undercover types she had met who worked for agencies such as the FBI and DEA, used a variety of identities, posing as everything from drug dealers to junk dealers. Their particular choice of cover depended on the crime they happened to be investigating.

A favorite cover for investigating gambling cases had been that of a salesman from some nondescript cereal or pharmaceutical company. The false identity allowed the investigator to hang out at seedy hotels and other establishments known to allow gambling rings to operate on the premises. Yes, Eve thought, if I were going to slip aboard undercover, I might choose sales.

"Are any of these people into sales?" she asked.

"Several are," Mike replied.

"Do you know what kind of sales?"

"I'm not really sure. I haven't paid that much attention. I think Larry Green is in drug sales—I mean prescription drugs," he added. “I think Moses Birnbaum is a jeweler, but I don’t know if it’s wholesale or retail. I don’t know if he works for someone or owns his own store.”

Eve was making notations by each name as Mike talked. These were things that could be checked out if she talked to them or eventually got to a phone.

“Evan Donitsky, I think he might be in sales too, but I’m not sure what type.”

They continued through the list, noting as much as Mike knew about each passenger next to his name. By noon, Mike had identified two other men he thought might be in sales, Calvin Ridge and Edward Amsterdam.

“Those are the two who supposedly ordered the sandwiches,” Eve said. She decided not to tell Mike about the beach or the conversation she had overheard. Even if he were not involved in the murders, he still couldn’t keep a secret. Anything she said would be all over the ship in no time. “Do you know what kind of sales or what company?”

“Insurance maybe,” Mike said. “I don’t know a lot about them. They seem nice enough.”

Eve seriously doubted the killer would have ordered sandwiches sent to his own cabin, but stranger things had happened. Obviously, someone had gone to a lot of trouble to get the cook out of the kitchen. Addison had gone to question them, and she planned to check them out too. By narrowing the list to men in sales, she had further reduced the number of suspects, but no one in particular stuck out as a killer. She was becoming discouraged, and she needed a break.

She left Mike still trying to remember as much as he could about each passenger, including conversations they had shared. He was jotting the relevant information on the full list and short list. She had made a copy of the list, circled the five names of the men believed to be in sales, and taken it with her. Her plan was to meet as many of them as possible, and she could think of no better time than lunch.

Addison looked up expectantly as she came into the dining room. "Any luck?" he asked.

"Nothing yet," she said. "How about you?"

"I talked to Ridge and Amsterdam. They said they never ordered the sandwiches and found them in their cabin when they got back. They just thought they were a complimentary snack and ate them. The empty plate was still there," he said.

"And the conversation?"

"They were nervous when I asked them about it, but they claimed not to recall having it. They said whoever overheard them must have misunderstood what was said. Of course, they wanted to know who the eavesdropper was," Addison said, smiling, "but I didn't tell."

"Thanks, I'm not looking forward to the next body being mine." She paused and then asked, "Why do you think they were so nervous?"

"I don't know. Perhaps they're no more nervous than anyone else is with all that's happened. But there were a couple of things that bothered me. Both are from Chicago, which is the right location. They apparently knew each other before the cruise and are traveling together, although they made their bookings separately to make it appear they weren't."

"Are they married?"

"Ridge isn't. Amsterdam is. He showed me pictures of his wife and kids."

"They're both big guys," Eve said. Addison nodded in agreement. They were both thinking that the men were capable of the strength required to lift Emory into the boat. If they were working together, it would help answer how so many things could have happened in such a short period of time—the murders of Flo and Tony, the wrecking of the communications system, the vandalizing of the boats, and Emory's murder.

"We'll have to keep an eye on them," Addison said. "I don't know of anything else we can do until we get a chance to check out their backgrounds."

Eve nodded in agreement, thinking she would have a chat with them herself. Perhaps Ridge would be friendlier in the daylight.

"How is Engstrum?" she asked, changing the subject.

"He's doing better," Addison said. "He's talking and starting to complain, always a good sign. White says he'll have a scar, but he'll be okay in a few days. He still can't walk around without getting dizzy or nauseated. White said he's got a severe concussion, but at least his skull wasn't fractured."

"White's turning into quite the healer," Eve said. "Speaking of healing, how's Vincent doing with the boat?"

"He's working on it. He says it will be patched by late this afternoon, but I'm not sure I want to chance going for another swim."

Eve nodded. The last thing she wanted was another opportunity to drown and be run down by a freighter or become shark bait. She glanced around the room. She thought she recognized the faces of some of the people who had made her short list of suspects. There was nothing about them that appeared suspicious. Eve sighed; it wasn't like the movies where the bad guys looked the part and the background music often signaled their approach. Most of the killers she had seen at trials she had covered had nothing particularly distinctive about them. They came in all shapes and sizes and from all walks of life. They lived in houses and apartment buildings, in quiet suburban neighborhoods and in decaying city slums. They raised families, and most dressed like everyone else in their income level. Most murderers killed people they knew and for fairly obvious reasons, which made it easier to determine who they were. Those who killed for a living were a different breed and far harder to find. For the money that was being offered, Eve was sure the people who had wanted Tony dead had been able to hire the very best.

"Engstrum thinks we should not risk another trip in an unsafe boat. He thinks it's time to take the *Clipper* into port and get help," Addison said, interrupting Eve's thoughts.

"He'll get away if we do that. It's exactly what the killer wants. He'll walk away from all this," she said, alarmed. "Even if we bring in the local police, I fear they will be no match, and the killer will have many more opportunities to disappear."

"At this point, Engstrum wants him off the ship. He's afraid for the rest of the passengers. The line's already looking at a potential for enough lawsuits to put it out of business without getting more people killed. He says we are flaunting all kinds of safety rules by not having functioning rescue boats or life jackets or a means of communication..." Addison's voice trailed off.

"But surely you don't think we should give up yet and let him walk away," Eve argued, her voice rising.

"No, of course not. I have a personal interest in catching the killer, but I can see his point. He thinks if we sail into port, we can still keep the passengers on board or at least make sure they don't leave the island until we have made sure they're not who we're looking for."

Eve thought for a time and then said, "With the kind of money the killer has at his disposal, he may have set up escape routes involving any number of these islands before he ever came aboard. If he didn't, who is to say he couldn't simply hire some native to take him to another island. You have to remember, we probably won't be the only ship docked there when we come into port. The killer could simply mingle with passengers from another ship and disappear that way."

"I agree with everything you're saying, but I don't think I'll be able to talk Engstrum out of sailing into Green Parrot Cay."

"When?"

"This afternoon."

"Then I don't have much time," she said, getting up from the table.

"To do what?" he asked.

"To narrow down my list of suspects," she replied.

She spotted Candy on the other side of the dining room sitting alone at one of the long tables and made her way toward her. Candy had been on the ship since the beginning of the cruise and probably knew most of the passengers. Eve reasoned that she did not consider her to be a suspect, at least not one on her short list, and, therefore, Candy might be quite helpful. After her initial somewhat negative impression of her, Eve had gradually concluded that depth, intelligence, and perhaps pain lurked beneath the light-hearted party-girl facade. Eve suspected Candy had assumed the image for the cruise. She remembered Candy's twisting of the absent wedding or engagement ring on her left hand. Sometimes people went on cruises to forget as much as they went on them to create wonderful memories. She had begun to suspect that Candy was here to forget.

"May I sit down?" Eve asked.

"Sure," Candy said, immediately placing the hands she had been studying back in her lap.

"I was wondering if you could help me," Eve said.

"Of course," Candy replied, interest registering in her lovely eyes.

"I'm not familiar with many of the passengers yet, having only recently gotten here and then with everything that's happened..." Eve's voice trailed off. "Well, I really haven't had a lot of time to mix with them. I need to know who some of them are, what they do—that sort of thing. But I don't want them to know I'm checking..." She paused again and then blurted out, "That I'm investigating them."

"I'll help," Candy said without hesitation. "I really hate just sitting here waiting and wondering who might be next. I took this trip to get away from some very unpleasant things that were happening in my life, and now I'm wondering if what I was escaping is as bad as what I seem to have gotten myself into. Who have you got?"

"Moses Birnbaum," Eve said, reading the first name on her list.

Candy smiled and looked across the room toward a short, bewhiskered, dumpy little man who looked to be pushing seventy.

"Probably not your man, unless he's in disguise," she said. "I think he suffers from gout, high blood pressure, and a variety of other ailments. I doubt that he would have the strength or the stamina to kill two people or sabotage the lifeboats."

"I think you're right," Eve said, crossing his name from the list. She spread her short list on the table in front of Candy, who bent over it rapidly scanning the names.

"I don't really know Amsterdam, Ridge, or Green very well, and I don't see them here now," she said. "Donitsky is that rather tall, good-looking man at the table behind you. The funny thing about him is that he almost always carries a canvas bag with him, even at meals. Makes you wonder what's in it."

Eve turned casually to look behind her, and a pair of intense green eyes met her gaze and then turned away.

"So much for casual surveillance," Eve said, reddening as she turned back to Candy.

"Don't worry about it. He probably thinks we're trying to decide if he's married. Men tend to think women are such empty vessels. Sometimes we promote the image, I'm afraid," she said, undoubtedly recalling their first meeting. "Perhaps you should do some serious flirting. I'll see if any of the others on your list are on deck and let you know."

Eve nodded her thanks and was about to move to Donitsky's table when he got up, picked up his canvas bag, and headed below deck toward his cabin. Eve watched the bag as he left. It was large enough and appeared to be heavy enough to hold a gun.

A few minutes later, Candy returned to announce that the others on the list were not on deck.

"Perhaps they ate before and have gone to their cabins to prepare for the afternoon on Green Parrot Cay," Eve said, half to her herself. Perhaps the preparations of at least one of them included a plan to escape.

CHAPTER NINETEEN

Green Parrot Cay lay like a dark, verdant dot off the bow of the ship. The greenery was outlined by a strip of sandy white beach, which grew larger as the *Clipper* sailed toward the harbor. The cay was the privately owned realm of a flamboyant expatriate American named Ernest Kellerman. Kellerman, now in his eighties, had left the United States in his youth to roam the world. He had joined the navy and served his country on a ship in the South Pacific. After his stint in the military, he had come to the Caribbean, bought a small freighter, and begun hauling freight and passengers back and forth among the islands.

On his trips, Kellerman often passed Green Parrot Cay, then an uninhabited island. Each time he passed it, he thought it was an island that he would like to own someday. It never bothered him that the reason it was uninhabited was that the nearly flat island consisted of mostly swamps and dense jungle. Even the natives stayed away because the insects seemed to grow larger and more vicious there than anywhere else in the Caribbean. Where the trees swayed lazily in the breezes on most of the Caribbean islands, the heavy air on Green Parrot Cay, for some unexplained reason, almost always lay motionless in the steamy heat.

Besides, the locals believed the island was haunted. If someone ventured in, they never came out, they claimed. Kellerman didn't believe in the local superstitions, nor did he worry about the amount of work it would take to make the island inhabitable.

By the early 1990s, Kellerman's freighter business had prospered, though he was anything but rich. Despite a continuing shortage of funds to finance much of anything, he had gone to the government of Saint Vincent with a proposal to lease the island for a dollar a year for ninety-nine years. He promised to turn it into a first-class resort.

In the beginning, the officials chuckled and scratched their heads, quite convinced that the American was crazy. They were less surprised by the miserly offer for the island than by Kellerman's desire to turn a swamp and jungle inhabited by nasty insects and poisonous snakes into a resort. Aside from it being the most uninviting place in all of the Caribbean, the officials knew Kellerman would have a hard time getting help to clear the jungle and drain the swamps because of the natives' belief that the place was haunted.

Most concluded Kellerman was a dreamer and that his plan was doomed to failure. But he persisted, and the officials concluded they had nothing to lose. They particularly liked the idea of an American pouring his own money into a useless island that would eventually revert to their ownership after it had been improved. Aside from the payment of the lease, they made Kellerman agree to invest a large percentage of his income in the island each year, something he would have done, anyway.

Kellerman was married to an American woman when he arrived in the Caribbean, but she soon tired of the back-breaking work of clearing the land and draining the swamps. She returned home where she eventually got a divorce. Before she left, Kellerman had already begun living with a native woman, who bore him five children, although he never married her.

Two children from his American wife returned to live with him. They and the children of his long-time companion helped him run the resort that had painstakingly taken shape at the edge of the jungle. Over the years, he had managed to clear a considerable portion of the island and to drain many of the swamps, but the Caribbean breezes, for some unknown reason, never seemed to find the place. According to several of the *Sun Clipper*'s passengers who had visited the island on previous trips, it was still one of the buggiest places in that part of the world.

It was hard to understand why anyone would spend the kind of money it cost to vacation there when the Caribbean was full of many more inviting places. But tourists paid top dollar to stay in one of Kellerman's thatched cottages and to stroll on his white beaches. An attraction undoubtedly was the exclusivity of the place, but even that was vanishing because Kellerman, never one to overlook a way to squeeze out more tourist dollars, had begun letting certain cruise lines include the island as a stop. So on the days when cruise ships anchored offshore, the nearly deserted hideaway overflowed with hundreds of noisy tourists who took over the beaches, commandeered the lounge chairs, and spread their towels under the thatched beach umbrellas. Others crowded the bar and single restaurant, leaving little place for the paying guests to find refuge.

Eve had heard the stories about the island and Kellerman, who was a local legend, and she looked forward to meeting him. On the advice of the other passengers, she armed herself with bug repellent from the ship's store. Although no one who had been there before seemed to like Green Parrot Cay, at this point they were happy at any chance to leave what many had dubbed "the ship of death."

The Overtons and several other passengers were already hovering near where the gangway would be lowered. Eve also found herself looking forward to having solid ground under her feet despite her concern that the killer would use this opportunity to slip away.

Earlier, both she and Addison had attempted to talk Engstrum into waiting one more day before allowing the passengers to debark, but he was unbending in his decision. He thought it was best for everyone's safety, and they were unable to dissuade him.

He had vetoed trying to take the launch into shore because Vincent's repairs were temporary at best, and Engstrum was not convinced the small boat would make it before it began leaking again. He also was not inclined to remain at sea when the ship did not have a single functioning lifeboat. It was simply too dangerous. Then there was the problem of the killer himself, who might be getting more desperate as time went on and who might strike again if he thought someone was getting too close. He had already killed Emory, possibly for that very reason. Engstrum reasoned he would rather allow the killer to escape than take the risk of letting anyone else die.

Yet another compelling argument for stopping at Green Parrot Cay was to restock their supplies. The cruise line had an agreement with Kellerman to use the island as a pickup point for food and other items shipped from the States and stored there. Providing storage for provisions and selling fresh water to the lines were among Kellerman's many profitable enterprises.

From his sick room, Engstrum ordered Vincent to take a head count of all passengers and crew who went ashore so they would know if anyone stayed behind that night. Under normal circumstances, the ship would have arrived early in the day so the passengers could spend the day and early evening before returning to the ship to sleep. Under normal circumstances, the ship would have sailed to the next island during the night and early hours of the following morning. But nothing was normal now, and Engstrum did not know when the ship would sail again or if it would at all. It was possible they would all be taken to Saint Vincent for questioning and detained. Much would depend on the instructions he and Addison received from the States.

Eve was relieved to see that no other cruise ship was anchored in the harbor so the killer would not be able to hide among its passengers and vanish. But she was concerned to see that several smaller boats were anchored offshore, within easy reach of someone who knew how to swim. After she shared her concerns about the increasing number of ways to escape, including commandeering one of the anchored pleasure craft, Engstrum ordered a crewman to keep an eye on the boats to make sure none of the passengers swam out to them. That took care of the part of the island they could see. However, Eve did not know what opportunities for escape might present themselves on the other side of the island. It was completely hidden from view. Engstrum hoped to solve that problem by asking Kellerman to provide some of his staff to help with surveillance.

The captain, his head swathed in bandages and looking like he was about to pass out, managed to make it to the deck in time to see the passengers go ashore. He was determined to go too, to meet with Kellerman and to avail himself of his phone.

As the last of the passengers was disembarking, Eve saw a white-haired man walking briskly up the dock toward them. He waved and smiled when he spotted the captain. Engstrum did his best to wave back, but he appeared in danger of losing his balance at even such slight motion.

"You should stay in bed," said Dr. White, who had lingered behind with his patient. "You're in no condition to be on your feet yet."

Eve and Addison also waited to accompany Engstrum. The next few hours would be critical in deciding what direction the investigation would take. They needed the captain to obtain Kellerman's cooperation.

Kellerman was tanned and his face wrinkled from years in the sun that made him look his age, but he walked with the speed and purposeful step of a much younger man. He was still quite handsome with a youthful figure, a full head of silver hair and the bluest eyes Eve had ever seen.

"What happened to you?" Kellerman asked as he extended his hand to Engstrum. "You look pretty awful."

"It's a long story," Engstrum began. "I'll fill you in after I find a place to sit."

They followed Kellerman up the beach toward an open-sided restaurant that overlooked the beach and were led to a table in the deserted dining room.

The warm expression on Kellerman's face had quickly changed to a look of genuine concern as he led Eve, Addison, and a visibly wobbly Engstrum to their seats. Engstrum collapsed onto a chair with a groan and waved Kellerman to a place across from him. After water and other refreshments were ordered and placed in front of them, Engstrum began his story with the murders and the events that had ensued.

Kellerman listened intently as Engstrum filled him in on all that had transpired and their search for the killer, whom they believed to be among the passengers.

"And now he's on my island?" Kellerman asked at last.

"I'm sorry, Ernie," Engstrum said apologetically.

Kellerman dismissed the apology with a wave.

"Well, he won't get off the island, that I can guarantee," Kellerman said with resolve. "But you hardly look like you're up to the task of tracking him down. Why don't you take your doctor's advice and stay in bed. I'll contact Sinclair, and Mr. Addison here can get ahold of his people. We'll take it from here," he said.

"Excuse me," Eve said, interrupting. "I think it is also important to make sure he can't hide on the island. He could put your guests at risk by posing as one in order to make his escape."

"My sons will help with the patrol," Kellerman said. "They know our guests."

"We'd better get started," Addison said. "I need to let my office and the FBI know what happened. They will want to know about Emory."

"I want to begin running checks on the passengers," Eve said, rising.

"Unfortunately, we are a small island and have only one phone line, but you are welcome to use whatever you need. Cell phones don't work here."

"About contacting the local authorities…" Engstrum began.

"If they ask why they weren't notified immediately, I'll tell them the phone was out of order. That is a frequent occurrence in these parts, anyway," Kellerman said. "Even if I did call them late today, they probably wouldn't get here until tomorrow."

Engstrum nodded. "I knew you'd help," he said.

"I just don't understand why you waited to come ashore or didn't send up a flare or something to get us to come out."

"The boats were sabotaged, the flares are gone, and the life jackets are either slashed or missing," Engstrum said, sighing deeply. "The killer's thought of everything."

Eve left to get the passenger list that she had hidden under the mattress in Addison's cabin. As she neared her old cabin, she thought about the extra shirt and shorts she had bought but had not yet worn, that lay in a dresser drawer. A change of clothes would make her feel better, she thought. The crewman who had been guarding the cabin was no longer in sight. He had apparently been pressed into duty on shore. In truth, there was no need to guard the cabin now because the bodies were gone, and the passengers were on shore.

Eve hesitated before opening the door and stepping inside. If the ship's store had been open, she probably would have passed on getting her clothes and would have simply bought something new. Being in the cabin where she had found the bodies of Flo and Tony was not a pleasant experience. The smell of blood and death still permeated the air, and she was tempted to leave.

The shower door was open, and she could see the brown stains that had dried on the walls. She moved quickly to the dresser and opened the second drawer where she had left her purchases. She grabbed the shirt and shorts with hardly a glance and was heading out the door to Addison's cabin when she looked at what she was carrying. The shorts, though white like her own, were not the ones she had bought, and the T-shirt had large green parrots on it instead of the *Sun Clipper* logo. In an instant, she recognized the shirt as one she had seen in Melinda's store in Bequia. She had admired it as it lay on the counter with Flo's purchases.

Eve felt waves of shock and fear wash over her. How had Flo's clothes ended up in her drawer and where were her own clothes? She swallowed, and as she held up the folded shirt and shorts, a note dropped to the floor. Her hands trembled as she opened it and read, "You admired the shirt in Bequia, so I wanted you to have it. The shorts are too small for me. See if they fit. Somebody pointed out your cabin, and I guess they were right because there's no luggage! Flo."

Eve gasped. It was like receiving a message from a ghost. Flo and Tony must have stopped by the cabin to leave the clothes after she had already gone on deck to watch the shooting of the cannons. Whoever the killer was must have followed them and killed them there. But why had everyone overlooked the clothing when the cabin was searched, Eve wondered, and then quickly answered her own question. No one had thought anything about an extra pair of shorts and a T-shirt in her drawer, and she had not looked in the drawer until now. She forced herself to return to the dresser, opened the drawer, and found her own shorts and shirt shoved to the back. She took them out and left the room, closing the door behind her.

"What are you doing?" The voice behind her startled her. Turning, she saw Addison walking toward her. "What were you doing in there?"

"I went to get my clean clothes, but look what I found," she said. "I think it will explain why Tony and Flo were in my cabin when they were murdered."

Addison looked at the note. "Where was it?"

"In the drawer with the shorts and shirt. After the bodies were found, I'm sure someone looked in the drawer, but no one knew these weren't mine. Flo and Tony must have dropped them off on their way on deck, but they never made it," Eve said. "Flo kept trying to loan me clothes to replace the ones the airline lost. The last thing she did before she died was something nice for me."

Eve felt tears welling up in her eyes. Addison put his arms around her and hugged her awkwardly. "Go change; I'll wait," he said.

"Why did you follow me?" Eve asked.

"I've told you before, I don't want you wandering around alone," he said gruffly.

"No one's here now. I'm probably safer here than on shore."

He said nothing for a minute as he turned the note over in his hands. "You would think so, but this person does not always do what we think he will do. Don't take chances. I've already lost three people I cared about."

CHAPTER TWENTY

Kellerman's description of the unreliable phone service proved to be true. After nearly twenty minutes of trying to get an island operator to put a call through to his office, Addison had just begun telling a colleague what had happened when the line went dead.

"This happens all the time," Kellerman said. "They'll get it fixed soon, or I'll send someone by boat to report the problem."

"We don't have that much time," Addison said. "Do you have a radio?"

"I do for emergencies, but I thought you weren't ready to call in the locals," Kellerman said.

Addison nodded. "How far is it to an island with a good phone system?"

"At least an hour by boat," Kellerman said. "I can have someone take you there."

Addison hesitated, weighing his options. Eve surmised that he was probably worried about leaving when he was the only person who had the training to go up against the killer. Even the captain, who was a decorated war hero, was in no condition to handle any rough stuff. He was barely able to walk and should have been in bed.

"Let's just wait and see if the phone service is restored. At least the office can begin to set a few things in motion," he said. Before the phone went dead, Addison had been able to give their location and to tell them that Tony and Flo had been killed. He had been about to add that Emory was dead as well, but the phone had died in midsentence.

They were in Kellerman's sparsely furnished office located in a white block building that overlooked the beach. The room lay off a club area that had a dance floor, dining room, and kitchen facilities. Rows of picnic tables were lined up under palm trees in front of the building. A volleyball net was set up further down the beach.

Eve had positioned herself near a window overlooking the area where tourists from the *Sun Clipper* had spread out their towels under the shade of thatched umbrellas. She was trying to see if anyone was missing, an impossible task when you considered there were fifty-six passengers on the ship.

Before they disembarked, Engstrum had asked them to remain together and to avoid exploring the island, for their own safety. Members of the crew were positioned to make sure the edict was obeyed. For most passengers, Eve thought the warning was probably unnecessary because they were frightened enough not to take chances wandering around alone. Eve knew it would be difficult to keep track of so many people if some decided to go exploring. If the killer made it into the jungle, he could slip away and perhaps find a way to get off the island.

Eve had not been paying strict attention to Addison's phone conversation, not until he uttered an oath when the line went dead. Despite Kellerman's assurances that this happened all the time, Eve was immediately suspicious and went to the window to see if she could tell whether anyone had left the beach. She reasoned that if the killer had made sure the ship's radio was broken and the boats were too leaky to get them to shore, it probably wouldn't take him long to disable the only phone line on the island. She slipped out of the building and walked to Charles, who stood guard nearest the building.

"Has anyone left the beach?" she asked.

"No, missy," he replied in his heavy island accent. "A few use the bathroom, that is all," he said, nodding in the direction of a portico at the side of the building. Eve saw the restroom sign, which pointed to entrances at the back of the building. She had a sinking feeling in the pit of her stomach as she began walking toward the restrooms. The women's restroom was the first one on the right, and the men's was the second on the right nearer to the back of the building. Both were next to the office.

She walked past the men's room door to a spot behind Kellerman's office where the phone line entered the building. As she suspected, the line had been neatly cut and to make sure it could not be easily spliced together, the killer had pulled the line from the telephone pole, clipped out the entire section, and dismantled the box. The whole operation had probably taken only a couple of minutes and had occurred right under their noses while they were in Kellerman's office. Eve saw footprints leading from the restrooms to where the wires had been cut and back to the restrooms. The shifting sand had already covered up most of the prints, making it difficult to discern whether they belonged to a man or a woman. She hurried back to the beach intending to ask Charles to try to remember who had just used the restrooms, but Charles was not there.

"Where's Charles?" she yelled at another crewman standing some distance down the beach.

He shrugged. "Maybe he went to the bar," he said.

Eve ran to where Charles had been standing to see if she could get an idea of which direction he had gone by looking at his footprints, but so many prints were visible near the front of the building that it was impossible to tell which were his. She knew she should tell the others what she had found, but she did not want to delay long enough for Charles to get away, not that she suspected him of being the killer. It was important to find him while his memory was fresh concerning who had gone to the men's room.

She ran to the bar and burst through the bamboo door hangings into the semidarkness of the room. It took a minute for her eyes to adjust before she could see that Charles was not among the *Sun Clipper* passengers at the bar or tables. Cecilia Overton was seated at one of the tables in the darkest corner of the room, waiting for her drink to come.

She waved at Eve and called her over.

"Have you seen Charles?" Eve asked breathlessly.

"No," Cecilia said. "Is something wrong? You look upset."

"No, I just need to find him. If you see him, please tell him I need him," Eve replied.

"Where will you be?" she asked.

"Probably at the office. It's near the restrooms," Eve added.

"Won't you stay and have a drink with me? You look like you could use one," Cecilia said.

"Another time," Eve said, waving as she rushed from the room.

Back on the beach, she retraced her steps to where Charles had been, but he had not returned, and no one knew where he had gone. She ran to the office and burst in on the group still waiting for the phone to come back on line.

"Don't waste your time," Eve said as she entered the room. "He's cut the line and smashed the box, so unless you can make some major repairs, the phone is not going to work. I would suggest you use the radio to call for someone to repair it before he destroys that too."

Addison looked startled. "He must have been outside the building while we were calling."

"Yes," Eve said. "He used a trip to the bathroom to get to the back of the building unnoticed. And the only person who might know who he is can't be found."

"What do you mean?"

"Charles was the closest to the restrooms and might remember who went in and out, but I can't find him. He's disappeared."

CHAPTER TWENTY-ONE

They took three of the crewmen from the beach and fanned out in search of Charles. No one on the beach had seen him after he left the spot in front of the restrooms. Before joining the search, Addison and Eve walked behind the building to examine the damage to the phone line.

"It can be fixed, but it is going to take time we don't have," Addison said, eyeing the missing line and the height of the pole.

The only person left in the office was Engstrum, who protested vociferously at being left behind, but he was in no condition to join in the search. He agreed to stay only after Addison convinced him he was needed to guard the radio, the only means of communication they had left.

After ten minutes of searching in the vicinity of the beach where Charles should have been and after checking a second time to make sure he was not in the bar, everyone met in front of the office. No one seemed to have a clue about Charles's whereabouts.

"He doesn't have a girlfriend on the island he might be visiting, does he?" Addison asked Kellerman, who had joined in with a gusto that belied his age.

"No, not that I know of," Kellerman said.

Vincent, who as always seemed to appear during every crisis and to make himself useful, had joined them in the office. "He has been seeing someone in Saint Lucia. He does not see anyone here," he offered.

"Perhaps we should search the rest of the island," Eve suggested.

Addison shook his head. "Perhaps we should stay here and let Charles find his own way back. I'm against anyone going off alone on the island. If Charles is able, he'll be back. And if he isn't, there probably isn't much any of us can do for him," he said darkly. "Our priority now has to be to set up communications and to get help."

"But Charles never left us when we were in trouble. He might need us now," Eve argued. She remembered Charles's reassurances and quiet strength as they clung to the sunken boat. It already seemed so long ago. "I for one want to make sure he is all right, and I will go by myself if no one else is up to it."

"I forbid you to go," Addison said, his voice rising in anger. "You can't go traipsing off by yourself. If something's happened to Charles, I will feel as badly about it as you, but there is no reason for you to suffer the same fate. The killer is still out there, and he is apparently feeling somewhat cornered."

"I don't think he feels cornered at all," Eve retorted. "He has been at least one step ahead of everyone, including the feds, this whole trip, and he continues to do just about anything he pleases. And I'm getting tired of it. I intend to find Charles, and I intend to find the killer," Eve said angrily. She turned her back on Addison and strode off down the beach. "Besides, no one died and made you God!" she yelled at him over her shoulder.

"Get back here, Eve! It's not safe!" Addison yelled. Several of the passengers who were within earshot looked anxiously at Addison.

Eve did not reply and kept on walking without looking back. Her anger and frustration carried her to the end of the beach that circled the small harbor. Eve saw a path leading into the jungle, and she turned left onto it and was immediately out of sight of the rest of the group. The jungle closed in on her almost at once, and she was treated to the sounds of birds, the chirruping of tree frogs, the hum of insects, and the rustling sounds made by animals who moved unseen through the thick brush. A variety of wild orchids seemed to thrive in the dank air, growing from the stumps of dead trees and mossy places. Brightly colored butterflies flew into the air as she walked. Under other circumstances, she would have found her surroundings quite enjoyable, but now growing feelings of foreboding robbed the scenery of its beauty. Those feelings had been building ever since she had found the phone line cut and Charles gone. Eve knew he would not desert his post without good reason.

Now she remembered what it was that had bothered her before. In her mind, she saw the footprints that had led from the back of the building. Most of the detail had disappeared in the soft sand, leaving only a smudge to show that someone had stepped there. But now she was sure they were different the second time she had viewed them with Addison and the others. On the second inspection, at least two sets of footprints instead of one had led from the cut phone line. Footprints also had led away from the building toward the jungle. She suspected some of the footprints probably belonged to Charles who had taken it upon himself to investigate. Perhaps he had gone to the restroom first to see if anyone was inside, and that explained why she had missed him when she looked for him on the beach before going to the bar. Charles must have decided to follow the footprints and perhaps had even seen the person who made them. If he had, he could identify the killer, and he was in grave danger.

She considered retracing her steps to the beach and the office so she could attempt to follow the footprints from the back of the office as Charles had probably done. But a few feet up the path, Eve found another path that intersected the one she was on. The path to the left ran parallel to the beach but was hidden from view by thick jungle growth. Eve suspected if she remained on it for a few minutes, it would circle back, and she would find herself directly behind the office again, perhaps on the path Charles had taken when he disappeared.

It was late afternoon, and the bugs were beginning to come out in force. They were especially vicious near the swampy areas that lay to the right of the path. She swatted at them as she walked and wished she had coated herself in the bug repellent she had left in her bag. After walking briskly for several minutes, she began moving ahead more slowly, looking left to see if she could see the building through the dense underbrush. A few yards further, she saw another path that intersected the one she was on. She guessed it must lead from the back of the building into the jungle. It wound around the edge of a swamp that was thick with vegetation growing from brackish black water.

Eve was having second thoughts about plunging more deeply into the jungle when something caught her eye. She was turning toward what appeared to be a piece of white material floating in the swamp on her right when she heard a sound behind her. Before she could turn around, she felt as if a building had been dropped on her head.

Fleeting thoughts came to her as her knees buckled, and she fell to the ground. The white object in the swamp was indeed a shirt, and the dark object that protruded from the sleeve was a man's arm. She knew even as she collapsed that Charles was dead, and she would be next.

Eve had no idea how long she had lain on the ground when she heard voices. They seemed to come from a great distance. She wanted to open her eyes and say something, but she found that she could not move or speak. Then she felt someone lifting her up and had the sensation of being carried before unconsciousness overtook her again.

CHAPTER TWENTY-TWO

Darkness had settled over Green Parrot Cay when Eve finally opened her eyes. As full consciousness came flooding back, she was relieved to find she was not lying in a swamp but on a bed in a small room in what she guessed was one of the guest cottages. The light from a table lamp covered with a bamboo shade lit the room in eerie streaks of yellow. What she could see of her immediate surroundings without moving her head, which throbbed in pain, was fashionably decorated with rattan furniture and green chintz. Bamboo shades covered the windows.

"You're finally back with us," Addison said, gathering her into his arms and holding her against him for a moment before laying her back down. "How do you feel? Dr. White said you would be all right, but I was afraid..." His voice trailed off.

"I feel terrible. How did you find me?"

"I couldn't let you go off alone, so I followed you," he said.

"Then you must have seen who struck me," Eve said, trying to push herself up on one elbow and wincing in pain as she turned her head to look into his eyes.

"I was too late. He got away."

"But you must have seen something."

"Nothing," he said.

Eve could not hide her disappointment.

"At least he did not have time to kill you like…" He stopped.

"You mean like he killed Charles."

Addison nodded sadly.

"How?" she asked.

"He used a garrote and then drowned him for good measure. He must be running low on bullets," Addison added bitterly.

"I can't believe you saw nothing. If you followed me, where could he have gone so quickly?"

"I don't know. The path leads to the beach and the bar. He probably ran when he heard me call you. At least he didn't have time to kill you as I'm sure he would have," he said.

"I guess I should be grateful for that, and I am. It's just that I had hoped…" She shook her head and felt pain pierce her like an arrow. "Poor Charles," she said, after she had recovered. "He must have tried to follow the tracks from behind the office. That's why he was there, I'm sure of it."

"What tracks?" Addison asked.

Eve told him about the tracks in the sand that had led from the back of the office toward the jungle. "When I saw them, I didn't realize that the reason they were so badly messed up was that two people had made them. I was so worried about Charles, I just wasn't thinking too clearly, and I also didn't realize until just before I was attacked that they hadn't been there when I first looked. That's why I'm sure Charles must have followed the killer who surprised and killed him." Eve's eyes filled with tears, and she wiped them away with the edge of the sheet. "If only I had remembered the tracks sooner…" she said.

"It probably wouldn't have saved Charles," Addison said. "The killer obviously struck quickly. Charles hadn't gotten very far."

He was probably right, Eve thought, but that was little comfort.

"By the way, how long was I out?"

"A couple of hours," Addison said. "You need to rest now, and I have to go. There are a lot of things that need to be done. Mike is outside, and he'll stay with you to make sure you are safe."

"But what is happening? Where am I? You just can't leave without telling me something."

Addison, who had gotten up from the side of the bed, sat back down again. He described their futile search of the jungle and the paths near where Eve was attacked. "Virtually everyone helped. Even the Overtons risked a few minutes of exposure to the elements to help," he said with a chuckle. After the search, most of the passengers had returned to the beach and enjoyed a buffet dinner that Kellerman had arranged before returning to the ship for the night.

"Everyone was accounted for," Addison said, anticipating her next question. "There is one other development, which I suppose was inevitable. After Charles was killed and you were attacked, Engstrum radioed the local authorities in Saint Vincent for help. They'll be here by morning. The connection was bad, but I also managed to get them to call my office and Emory's. Both agencies are sending men to the island. I expect they will be here by late tomorrow. The phone company is on its way, but Kellerman said not to hold our breaths until the lines are repaired. And finally, you're in one of his guest cottages. We felt it was best to keep you here for tonight. Now I have to go, but I'll be back."

He kissed her on the cheek, seemingly embarrassed by his own show of affection. "I don't know what I would have done if anything happened to you."

Eve thought she detected tears in his eyes as he turned to walk away. "Jerry," she called. He stopped near the door and turned toward her. "Thanks for saving my life," she said. "And please hurry back."

"I will," he said, smiling.

Mike came in and pulled a chair up beside the bed. He looked very tired, and Eve was relieved that he said very little after he got his initial polite inquiries as to the state of her health out of the way. She turned her back to him and tried to doze off, but the throbbing pain in her head kept her awake.

Later, Dr. White came in to examine his latest patient.

"I'm considering going back to medical school to become a G.P." White quipped. "Or maybe I should consider pathology. I want to make sure I'm certified before my next cruise."

Eve laughed and then decided it hurt to laugh. "Do you think you'll ever take another one after this?" Eve asked.

"Why, sure," he said. "I haven't been this much in demand since I made the mistake of offering free dental exams to the inhabitants of a homeless shelter. I had to stop doing it because my dental assistants threatened to quit. They were afraid they'd get AIDS or lice or something equally unpleasant. My practice suffered when my paying patients quit coming because they were afraid they'd be mugged coming to the office." White laughed again.

"And what's the verdict?" Eve asked as White alternated between probing her head and waggling his finger back and forth in front of her face.

"In medical terms, you've got a goose egg," he said, apparently enjoying his Marcus Welby role.

"I didn't need you to tell me that. I can feel it."

"There's no fracture, you were lucky there, but you've definitely got a concussion. Rest is the best cure for that."

"Can you give me aspirin or something for the headache?"

"I'd rather not just yet. If you can tough it out until tomorrow, I'll see what I can come up with then. Don't want to be sued for malpractice," he said with a twinkle in his eye.

Eve got the distinct impression that White was enjoying being a vital part of the investigation. Between treating their injuries and acting as forensic pathologist, he had certainly earned their respect and gratitude. Eve thought the line ought to let him travel free in the future, maybe make him an honorary crewman or medic. She would add that to her growing list of recommendations.

After White left, Eve lay on her side facing the wall. She could hear Mike's breathing become heavier as he dozed in the chair that was now positioned near the door. She too was tired, but she was afraid to sleep, so she lay awake in the semidarkened room for several hours before sleep finally came.

Eve guessed it must have been in the early morning hours when she was awakened by movement in the room and low whispers. The light had been turned off, and the room was dark, so she could not see who had come in. She heard the door close and felt the light cover being pulled back on her bed. Without a word, Addison slid into the bed and slipped his arms around her. She turned toward him and nestled her head against his bare chest.

"I thought you would never come," she said.

"I'm here now," he replied, bending to kiss her lips before they made love.

CHAPTER TWENTY-THREE

Addison was gone, and the room was empty when Eve awoke. She sat up slowly, trying not to jar her head any more than simple movement required. She stretched and decided that she felt decidedly better all over; even her head no longer reeled with pain when she moved it. The sexual release of the night before was better therapy than any pain killer. They had made love with an intensity and abandon of two people who had found themselves alone together during a lull in a war. There was good reason for this reaction as recollections of the events of the last three days flooded her thoughts. An assassin had declared war on members of the cruise who got too close, and the body count was rising.

Switching to happier events, she viewed the rumpled bed and tried to put the night's activities into perspective. She knew about shipboard romances from friends who had come back starry-eyed only to find that the Prince Charming of the cruise never wrote or called. The affairs usually ended abruptly when the reality of home and jobs caught up with the lovers. She had planned to guard herself against such involvement, but here she was, feeling and acting on a very strong attraction to a man she had thoroughly disliked three days ago.

She wondered if her feelings for Addison, which she was not yet ready to call love, were entirely borne out of the fear and uncertainty that had surrounded them throughout the cruise. Under normal circumstances, the pampered life on a cruise ship often spawned romance, but this bore no resemblance to a normal cruise. It was difficult to gauge the true depth of feeling between them, but she knew she didn't want anything to happen to him, and he was obviously quite protective of her. They had formed an unspoken bond in the midst of the craziness. They cared about each other, Eve thought.

Enough analysis, she told herself; she knew so little about him. She would have time to analyze their relationship later. At the moment, she was curious about what was happening, and she was also feeling a little hungry, which she took as a sign of returning good health.

Her now muddy and stained clothes were strewn on the floor next to the bed, and she had no desire to get into them again. She longed to take a warm shower and to put on clean clothes. She had already found a bathroom off the bedroom in the night, but unfortunately no one had left any clothes in the closet or single dresser that was pushed against the wall. She had already checked.

Well, she could have at least half of her wish, she thought, padding to the bathroom wrapped in a bedsheet. The warm water felt wonderful as she soaked under the shower. She had felt a little dizzy to start but was beginning to feel better when she realized that she was no longer alone in the room. Through the drawn shower curtain, she could see the outline of a man.

Summoning all of the strength she could muster, Eve screamed at the top of her voice.

"Eve, it's okay. It's only me," Mike said. "I just stuck my head in to make sure you were okay. Don't scream."

Eve stopped screaming in time to hear the bedroom door open with a crash as someone charged through it. Then she heard Mike yelp in pain.

"Are you okay, missy?" It was Vincent's voice. Now there were two men in the bathroom.

"I'm fine, but would you all get out and let me finish my shower."

"I'm sorry, missy. I heard you scream," Vincent said apologetically.

Eve wrapped the plastic shower curtain around herself and peered out at both of them.

"I just came to make sure you were okay," Mike repeated for Vincent's benefit. "You didn't have to punch me, Vincent."

"I don't know why you are here," Vincent said.

"Well, that's settled, and if both of you will please leave, I will get out and get dressed," Eve said.

"Mr. Jerry said for me to bring you these," Vincent said, laying a clean change of clothes on the sink. It was yet another *Sun Clipper* shorts and top bought at the ship's store.

"Thank you. That was very thoughtful," she said, noting that Vincent had dropped his usual formality and was now calling Addison by his first name, which she surmised was a sign of acceptance.

Both men left, but Eve guessed Mike was stationed outside her door and found her assumption correct when she opened it a few minutes later.

"Dr. White said you should stay in bed," Mike admonished.

"Make me," Eve retorted as she brushed by him and headed toward the beach.

"Jesus, Eve, you'll get me in trouble again. I've already got enough problems."

Eve threw him a glance that would kill. "Where were you when Charles disappeared?"

His face blanched, and he looked uneasy. "I've already told Addison; I was in one of the guest cottages…with someone."

"Who? Candy was on the beach when I walked by."

"Someone else," he said. "I really don't want to talk about it."

"If you had been where you were supposed to be, you might have seen Charles leave. You might have seen who followed him into the jungle. You might even have saved his life. Is there anything or anyone you won't screw?"

Mike didn't answer. Eve wasn't sure if he was angry or sad. He had withdrawn, and his black eyes seemed to sink into his head. Eve knew he probably had not had much sleep the night before, having been pressed into service to guard her door for at least part of the night, but she did not feel sorry for him. She didn't know if Mike could have saved Charles, but the possibility was very good that he would have seen something. As it was, no one was paying attention, and now kind Charles was dead, and they were no closer to finding out who the killer was…unless it was Mike, Eve thought. He had the opportunity, and he hadn't offered the name of anyone who could substantiate his alibi for where he was when it happened. His name also ended in a vowel, which should have automatically put him on her short list of suspects. Only she really didn't think Mike was right for the part of cold-blooded killer. A conniving ad man, an unscrupulous Casanova perhaps, but probably not a hired assassin. But money was always motive enough to tempt weak people to change.

The cottage where Eve had spent the night overlooked the white beach, and she found it was only a short walk to the office. She noticed that a new boat was in the harbor, and she assumed it had brought the police from Saint Vincent.

Some of the guests were already assembling at the tables in front of the office/dining-room building. Breakfast was being served, and she assumed the meal ashore had been arranged to provide the police with access to the passengers.

As she approached the office, Addison came storming out. "I can't believe this. They are arguing about jurisdiction. We've got three stiffs in a locker on the ship and one in cold storage here, and they are arguing about who has jurisdiction." He shook his head in seeming disbelief.

"It's the tropics," Eve said, trying to calm him. "Come, relax a bit. We're on vacation," she said, hoping he would see the humor in her remark.

"Why are you out of bed?" he said, turning his piercing blue eyes on her.

"I was hungry," she replied.

"You were curious," he said accusingly.

"That too."

Eve braced herself for an angry lecture, but Addison's mood changed to one of resignation. He threw up his hands and indicated a place at one of the picnic benches for the three of them to take their places.

"Who does have jurisdiction?" Mike asked.

"They say they have it here and can investigate Charles's death, but they don't think they have jurisdiction to investigate the other deaths. They don't know who does. The ship belongs to an American line that is registered in Panama, and no one is exactly sure where the other three were killed. We think it was near Bequia, but we don't know for a fact. Whoever committed these killings must be enjoying every minute of the confusion."

"But if they begin with Charles's death, which is the freshest, and find the killer, they will essentially have solved the other three," Eve said. "In any case, I think they should get started on the one they know is theirs and worry about the others when the jurisdictional question is settled. Meanwhile, if they have a pathologist on the island, perhaps autopsies should be started."

"My argument exactly, but they aren't convinced. I had to get out of there before I thoroughly lost control." Addison rubbed his face with his hands as if to ease his tiredness and frustration.

"Have some juice," Eve said, pouring what looked like papaya juice into his glass. "You might as well have breakfast. This is going to be another long day in the tropics."

Addison drank his juice and picked at his breakfast before leaving the table and going back inside. To Eve's disappointment, he did not suggest that she accompany him, instead telling her once more that she should spend the day in bed, something she had no intention of doing. His only indication of their romantic night together was a gentle squeeze of her hand under the table just before he left. She wondered if he might be having regrets and had come to the conclusion that his actions were just one more bit of craziness in this already out-of-control situation. She hoped that was not the case because her feelings for Jerry Addison at that moment were stronger than any she had felt in the nearly five years since her divorce. During those years she had dated a variety of men and had frequently wondered if she would ever really care about someone again in that special way. The disappointment and hurt associated with divorce tended to do semipermanent damage to certain feelings. It was so hard to let go again. It was even harder to trust. She liked what she was feeling for Addison. She would hate to think the feelings were not reciprocated.

CHAPTER TWENTY-FOUR

After Addison left, Eve finished her breakfast and decided to continue investigating on her own. She moved to the next table to mingle with some of the passengers. The Canadian nurses, among those sitting there, were full of questions about the turn of events. She suspected they were only seeking confirmation of what they already knew because Mike would have told them. The only one who had little to say was Ulrika, recovered from her swim but still seemingly shaken by the deadly events. Or was she simply a very good actress?

The Overtons also had been sitting at the next table with their backs to Addison and Eve during breakfast, and Eve suspected they had overheard enough of their conversation to know what had transpired. Everyone was solicitous and inquired about her head injury. Eve assured them she was feeling much better. In fact, she tried to make it sound as if she were better than she really felt. The nurses had been unaware of the current argument over police jurisdiction until now and were concerned that it might mean they would be stranded on Green Parrot Cay for some time.

"Your guess about what happens next is as good as mine," Eve said.

"They really should let us leave," Oliver Overton said. "This trip has been a disaster, and I, for one, am ready to get home." His wife nodded in agreement.

"We have writing to do, and we might as well get to it," Cecilia said. "I see no point in staying here any longer."

"I can't imagine what you'll write after a cruise like this," Eve said. "What happened here would hardly lend itself to a light, bright travel piece. It's got more of the makings of a whodunit," she added.

"You're right, of course," Cecilia said. "But we'll have to write something. *The Overton Guide to Travel* has another edition due out soon after we get back. Our readers look forward to positive travel tips. I admit this will be hard to write."

"Don't you usually have a couple of months' lead time on a monthly magazine?" Eve inquired.

For the first time, Cecilia seemed slightly flustered and looked at her husband. "You're right about that," Oliver said. "But I'm afraid we let things get behind before we left. You know, family problems and such."

"I didn't think you had a family," Eve said.

"We don't have children. We have in-laws," Overton said, but he didn't elaborate.

"I guess everyone knows about those kinds of problems," Eve said. "I'd love to see a copy of the magazine if you have one with you."

"I'm afraid we didn't pack one. But if you give us your address, we'll send you a copy when we get home," Oliver said, his face brightening. "We could enclose a calendar too."

"That would be nice," Eve replied.

Turning to include the nurses in the conversation, Eve said, "I hear all of you helped in the search yesterday."

They nodded. "We were on the beach when Jerry Addison started yelling for help," Candy said. "We all went flying."

"Yes, Oliver and I had been in the bar," Cecilia said, "but then you knew that. You had seen us there earlier," she reminded Eve. "You know how I hate the sun, but we helped too when we were asked. But nobody saw anything except poor Charles's body, of course."

Everyone at the table became still. Eve saw nothing to alert her suspicions in their sincere facial expressions that mingled grief and shock with a degree of curiosity.

Turning to Candy, she said, "I'm sorry Mike had to spend some of his time keeping an eye on me last night."

"Yes, he was on duty all afternoon and night. He seemed pretty tired this morning."

Eve noticed that Mike had left after breakfast without saying anything to Candy. "Where do you suppose he is now?" Eve asked, pretending to look around for him.

"I have no idea, and I really don't care," Candy said, disgust giving her voice an edge.

Eve eyed her but said nothing. She wondered if Candy knew that Mike's watch at her room did not start until the early morning hours.

Eve said her good-byes and moved to the next table where two of the men she had identified as potential suspects were drinking their second cups of morning coffee. At least one had opted for something stronger and was already feeling the effects. She noticed that Evan Donitsky still had the ever-present canvas bag next to him. As she sat down, she pretended to clumsily bump it. It felt heavier than it looked and thumped on the bench.

"I'm sorry, I hope I didn't break anything," she said. "It sounds like you've got rocks in there."

Donitsky eyed her. His gaze was not friendly. "Just some shells. I collect them."

"I'm Eve. I don't think we've officially met."

"I know who you are," he said, edging himself and the bag away from her. Donitsky spoke with a trace of an accent—Russian, perhaps. Eve felt a twinge of fear when she looked into his ice-green eyes. She wondered if they were the eyes of the killer who had nearly finished her in the swamp. Measuring him up, she judged him to be large enough and strong enough to have been physically capable of lowering the lifeboat, placing Emory's body in it, and hoisting it back up.

"So, Evan," she said, assuming a friendliness she did not feel, "what kind of work do you do?"

"I'm into sales," he said.

"What kind?" she asked.

"I don't think that is any of your business," he hissed.

"Now, Evan," the man sitting across the table from him said, taking a sip from a bloody mary, "no point in being unfriendly. We're all a bit on edge here. My name's Green, Larry Green," he said, extending a fleshy hand to Eve. "I'm into sales too—pharmaceuticals. I have some customers in this part of the world. Fortunately, not all the natives believe in voodoo cures." He chuckled, the only one at the table to laugh at his attempt at humor. "I like to combine a vacation with servicing my accounts. Looks like you could have used a little voodoo protection yourself," he said, eyeing the lump on Eve's head.

She smiled, wondering how she could check his credentials. Green, like Donitsky, was a large, strong man, but she wondered if he were capable of the strength required to lift Emory's body and to perform the other tasks, including sabotaging the lifeboats. Unless Emory had climbed into the lifeboat himself, someone would have had to lift him. Killing Charles also would have required strength unless he was caught by surprise, which he may have been. Otherwise, he would have struggled with his assailant.

Green was a smooth talker, a conman, she thought, but, then, wasn't the ability to con people a requirement of sales work? She tried to engage Donitsky and Green in conversation about their jobs, their homes and families without raising suspicion, but though Green spoke at length, Eve had no way of verifying the truth of what he said. Donitsky clammed up, providing her with little more than an uneasy feeling, and she still hadn't found a way to look inside his bag.

Eve decided to find Ridge and Amsterdam. In her mind she went over what she already knew about them. They both sold insurance, shared the same cabin, knew each other but were not keen on letting others know they had known each other before the trip. Mike said they had made their reservations separately and claimed to have been paired up by the travel agent who booked their cruises. They had been together on the beach where Addison, Emory, and Tony had met in Bequia. Then there was that strange conversation Eve had overheard. They had gotten the sandwiches that had lured the cook away from the kitchen the night Flo's hands had been cut off, though they said they hadn't ordered them. They were strong enough to have lifted Emory into the boat. Another point was, like Tony and Flo, both were from Chicago. That made for a lot of interesting coincidences.

Eve had seen them earlier, and now she looked for them again, but they had left their table, and she did not see them on the beach. She imagined the pair sneaking through the jungle, plotting a way to leave the island. However, if that were the case, there was little she could do but trust that some of the guards Kellerman had posted would intercept them.

For the most part, the other passengers she talked to appeared quite innocent and thought she was only being friendly. By the time she had gotten around to the fourth table, most of the passengers were heading for the beach. Eve walked among them chit-chatting and storing the information she gathered for future reference. She found few inconsistencies.

At the end of an hour, she had serious suspicions about Donitsky, Green, Ridge, and Amsterdam, but they were overshadowed by the nagging feeling that she had missed something. She couldn't for the life of her remember what it was. Annoyed by her inability to remember, she blamed her mental slowness on the blow to her head and her pounding headache. Eventually, she gave up trying to recall what seemed out of place. At least the nausea had passed, and she could focus her eyes without seeing two of everything.

She trudged back across the sand to the office to see what was new with the investigation. Engstrum met her at the door. He was looking somewhat healthier than he had the day before and told her his headache had lessened, but he seemed quite depressed.

"We look worse than some of the soldiers and seaman who fought in the war. I've never had so many walking wounded on a cruise, let alone three dead. Perhaps it's time to rethink my career and consider a return to the military. It was safer," he said, regaining a little of his old humor.

"Why did you leave the military?" Eve asked. It was a question she had been wondering about since she met him.

"I hated the fighting, the killing, the bloodshed," Engstrum said. "When one war ends, another begins. I wanted to get away from it. I never wanted to kill anyone or see anyone killed again. That's why I don't own a gun or any weapon. I started out believing I was strong and ended up deciding I was too weak for war, so I left. I wonder if my weakness here has caused more pain and loss of life."

"You had nothing to do with what happened. You were just unlucky that it happened on your ship. Don't get discouraged," Eve said. "We'll get through this. No one can possibly blame you for anything."

"I disagree. I should have gotten the authorities involved right away. Charles would be alive—maybe even Emory. You wouldn't have been hit over the head, nor, for that matter, would I," he said bitterly. "I clearly failed to make the correct decision."

"I don't think so. You were trying to get to a phone to call for help when the launch sank. You had no idea that was going to happen. Besides, I think you should stop second-guessing what should have been done. The question is what is to be done now."

Engstrum sighed deeply. "They are going to question the passengers concerning Charles's death and the assault on you. As for the other deaths, they are awaiting a ruling from one of their superiors on the question of jurisdiction. I think they are hoping the FBI or some other agency will investigate the other murders. You surely can't blame them. They can't have had experience investigating what appears to be a Mafia hit."

When Eve left Engstrum, he was still visibly depressed by the turn of events. She had been unable to shake his belief that he was to blame, at least for Charles's death and the assault on her.

Eve spent most of the rest of the day on the beach going from group to group to see what she could learn about the passengers. She left only once after lunch when she was called for questioning. The Saint Vincent policeman identified himself as James Monroe, "just like your president."

Eve could offer Monroe little new information. She described how she had been struck over the head from behind just as she had spotted Charles's body in the swamp. "And you did not hear or see anything?" Monroe asked. Eve shook her head, and after a few more questions, she was excused.

During the afternoon, she saw Addison occasionally go in and out of the office, but he did not stop to talk to her. She did not seek him out because she had no news to cheer him. When he appeared at dinner, he looked extremely tired.

The wind had picked up, and the dinner had been moved inside to keep sand from blowing into the food. Addison informed her that the arrival of the investigators from the States had been delayed a day by a tropical storm that had struck the islands further north with gale-force winds. It had also whipped up the winds here. She suspected the delay was one of the reasons he was in such ill humor.

After dinner, the passengers returned to the ship, and members of the crew organized crab races for the evening's entertainment. Participation in the races, often a highlight of the cruise second only to the firing of the cannons, was half-hearted at best. No one was in the mood for games. Though Eve did her best to enthusiastically cheer on her crab, aptly dubbed Lost Luggage by the crew, it turned in a performance worthy of its name. It got lost in the circle and came in last.

Afterward, Engstrum made a brief appearance to let the passengers know that the investigation was continuing. "If the investigators from the States do not arrive by tomorrow, the plans are to sail for Saint Vincent," he said. "That is all I can tell you, but I promise to keep you informed."

Eve decided to call it a night. Because her condition had improved, she turned down Kellerman's offer of the cottage for another night and returned to the ship with the other passengers.

CHAPTER TWENTY-FIVE

An hour after Eve had gone to bed, Addison joined her in the narrow bunk, kissing her gently and taking her in his arms. Their lovemaking was brief and more restrained than it had been the night before, in part because of the limitations imposed by the small bed and their mutual exhaustion. But it was no less exhilarating. They fell asleep almost immediately afterward.

Eve guessed it must have been between two and three in the morning when she awoke with a start and sat bolt upright in her bed. Her subconscious, which tended to be highly active when she slept, having provided her with some of her best investigative inspirations in the past, had sorted the bits of information she had collected. The missing pieces had fallen into place. The solution that had so eluded her was now staring her in the face.

It was clear to her who had committed the murders and had nearly succeeded in killing her on two occasions. Everything fit. She knew why and how the murders had been accomplished without anyone seeing them or any suspicions being aroused. She also knew where the gun had been hidden so it would not be found during their searches of the ship. If it was where she thought it was, the murderer still had it close at hand. Even if the weapon had been disposed of, the killer remained in a powerful position.

Without a doubt, something had to be done immediately. Logic as well as the subconscious nudging that had awakened her told her that the assassin was making plans to escape. It had to be tonight because the risk of being discovered tomorrow by the FBI loomed large. The agents would know him, possibly not on sight because although Eve had never seen him before the cruise, she knew that he was traveling in disguise. Surgery might have altered his features, but his fingerprints would not lie. They were likely on file with law enforcement. But how had Emory gotten close enough that the killer felt it necessary to get rid of him? Even with an altered appearance, he must have feared there was something else about him that would give him away. Once the feds arrived, she reasoned, the chances for escape would lessen greatly. He had to leave tonight to reduce his risk of being caught.

Eve considered waking Addison but decided against it. He was exhausted, and she could conduct her own little experiment first to make absolutely sure she was right before seeking his help. She slipped from the bed, pulled on her clothes, and let herself out of the cabin without making a sound.

To Eve's disgust, she found the crewman who was supposed to guard that part of the corridor asleep with his back resting against the wall. For the moment, however, this lapse in security suited her purposes because it meant she would not be interrupted. Barefooted, she stepped over his legs and moved soundlessly down the corridor to the cabin that was across from her old one. She knocked and waited, but as she suspected would be the case, no one answered. She had decided if anyone came to the door, she would make up an excuse about being frightened and looking for help. She was reasonably confident that the ruse would allow her time to get away. Now there might be no need for deception.

Cautiously, she pressed down on the latch and eased the door open. The light from the corridor provided enough illumination for her to see that the cabin was empty. Fearing she was already too late, she closed the door quietly and ran down the corridor and up the stairs to the deck. The gate to the gangway that led to the dock was open. No one was guarding it. That was odd but not unexpected. Straining her eyes, she looked along the dimly lit dock but saw no movement. The killer had already left the ship and made his way to shore.

She hesitated, knowing she should get help, but precious moments would be lost. Throwing caution aside, she hurried down the dock toward the beach, trying to make as little noise as possible. She paused as her feet touched the sand, not knowing which way to go. She tried to think what she would do next if she wanted to escape. There was Kellerman's yacht, which she had passed anchored to the dock, but Kellerman had taken pains to disable it so no one could hot-wire the motor and drive off. She looked away from the dock along the shoreline but saw no one there.

In the moonlight, she scanned the boats that bobbed at anchor. They looked the same as they had earlier in the day. Nothing appeared unusual, but she had a feeling she was missing something. She ran along the beach and finally saw what she was looking for. The surf had not yet had time to erase the footprints at the water's edge. She looked at the yacht that was anchored about thirty yards off the shore in a direct line from where the footprints entered the water and thought she saw movement on deck. Then she heard muffled voices.

She slipped into the water without so much as a splash and used the powerful breast stroke that she had developed at high-school swim meets to move swiftly and soundlessly through the water. She had no idea what she would do when she arrived at the boat, but she felt compelled to do something before time ran out. As she swam, for some unexplainable reason, she thought of a comic-book character she had admired as a child and was momentarily amused by the similarity between the impossible task she faced and those accomplished by her childhood heroine, Sheena, Queen of the Jungle. Sheena was always rescuing captives from evildoers. As a child, Eve had frequently played the role of Sheena, acting out fantastic scenarios in the woods behind her house. Now the fantasy was real.

Within minutes, she was at the side of the yacht. Circling soundlessly, she tried to determine what had happened to the young couple she had seen on it during the day. Pulling herself up high enough, she peered through a porthole into the only lighted cabin. They were huddled in a corner, gagged and tied securely with rope. Eve surmised they had been kept alive to be used as hostages should the killer be caught and have to bargain his way out. Once they were no longer needed, Eve knew they would be killed. So far, the killer had left no witnesses. She heard movement on deck and suspected that she had only minutes left to do something before the engine started up and they sped away to some unknown destination.

She considered yelling at the top of her voice but feared she might be silenced so quickly no one would hear her cries. Instead, she moved to the ladder at the stern and eased herself up the steps, hoping the water that ran from her clothing would not make enough noise to give away her presence. The movement she had heard was coming from a spot near the bow. Someone was preparing to start the engine. Soundlessly she moved toward the steps to the cabin where she had seen the couple, hoping that she might be able to free them. As she crept forward, she looked for something she might use as a weapon and spotted a pole with a hook used for docking. It would be no match for a gun, but it was better than nothing, she thought. With luck, she might find a knife or even a heavy cooking pot if she could make it to the galley undetected.

Clutching her weapon, she crept quietly down the stairs and through the half-open door into the cabin. Oliver Overton was bending over the couple, apparently making sure their ropes were secure.

"It's you," he said with a snarl as he turned and saw Eve. Overton was no longer swathed in layers of clothing and had removed his straw hat. His skin was unusually pale, and the scratches Flo had made on his arms and chest in her futile struggle to survive were pinkish lines. Eve guessed Oliver was suffering from what one would describe as "prison pallor" rather than a skin condition caused by an allergic reaction to the sun.

"What's this, Oliver, no longer worried about your skin?" Eve asked. "And get a load of those tattoos. You must have gotten them in the joint." Especially mesmerizing on his sinewy torso was one of a fire-spouting dragon writhing around a heart with the word "Mom" in the middle.

As he took a step toward her, she lunged with the docking pole and plunged it into his midsection as hard as she could. He "harrumphed" and doubled over but remained standing. She knew she had stopped him only temporarily by knocking the wind out of him. Before he could recover, she raised the pole again and brought it down with a thud on his head.

"Just a little payback, Oliver," she said as he slumped to his knees. She whacked him once more on the side of his head.

She heard Cecilia on the stairs and knew her luck was about to run out as the woman burst through the doorway. "What have you done?" Cecilia yelled as she looked from Eve to Oliver, who was trying to catch his breath and get to his feet. Blood was running down his cheek from the head wound inflicted with the pole.

Under other circumstances, Eve would hardly have recognized Cecilia. Her transformation was even more startling than Oliver's. She was wearing shorts and a T-shirt and looking younger and far more robust without the hat and billowy layers of white clothing that had engulfed her.

Equally fascinating were the number of tats that also covered much of her body. Some appeared to match those of Oliver. A sign of true love? Eve marveled. If there had been more time, Eve could have stared at the intricacies, but Cecilia was reaching into the bag that she always carried with her. When she pulled her hand out, she held the gun Eve had known would be there.

"Here, I used to think you carried tons of sunscreen in there," Eve said. "I have to compliment you on your disguises. You had us all fooled." Eve's voice sounded more confident than she felt. There was no doubt in her mind that Cecilia was about to blow a hole in her the size of a cantaloupe. But it was too late to awaken Addison now. She heard Oliver Overton, or whoever he was, struggling to his feet behind her. In a second, life as she knew it would be over.

"Guess you two must have met in prison," Eve said, moving to her right.

"Stay the fuck right there, smartass," Cecilia said. Even her voice had changed. It was hard and no longer refined.

"What language, Cecilia. I never thought you had it in you," Eve chided.

"How did you know? How did you find us?" Cecilia asked, waving the gun at Eve.

"I guess it was the travel magazine," Eve said, moving to her right again as she spoke.

"What about it?"

"Do you really want to know?" Eve asked, trying to buy a little more time to think of something. "Well, Cecilia, or whatever your name is, most editors of small magazines don't put out monthly editions; they put out issues. They also would bring copies with them to show them off and perhaps get new subscribers. You didn't have any," Eve said. "Tonight, I remembered that Oliver wasn't in the bar when I went to look for Charles. You were the only one there, Cecilia, because Oliver was busy getting rid of poor Charles.

And you had to improvise when you killed him, didn't you, Oliver, because Cecilia had the gun in her bag. Time was short, so you used a garrote made from the telephone wire you had just cut."

"We should have killed you right away. I told him that," Cecilia said.

"Oliver, you should have listened to her," Eve said. "But it's too late; the cavalry is on the way."

"You're bluffing," Cecilia said. "You're on your own, but, in any case, you're dead," she said, raising the weapon to fire.

While they were talking, Oliver had managed to get to his feet and began to advance toward Eve from behind.

As Cecilia pulled the trigger, Eve dove to her right. She landed in a heap on top of the young couple, expecting the next deafening blast would surely end her life and maybe theirs too. Instead, she heard a sound behind her like the air being let out of a tire. She scrambled to get to her feet before Cecilia could fire again or Oliver could leap on top of her.

As she rolled off the couple and began to rise, she caught sight of Cecilia's horror-stricken face. She was not looking at Eve but at Oliver who was sinking to the floor, a look of surprise on his face. His hands were trying futilely to stem the flow of blood spurting from a gaping wound in the middle of the tattooed heart where the bullet had entered his chest. Cecilia let out a shriek, and the gun went limp in her hand as she ran to help Oliver. The fatally wounded man continued to stare at her as he fell forward onto his face.

Eve sprang to her feet and grabbed the boat hook that lay on the floor. She swung it against Cecilia's arm as hard as she could. The gun fell from her hand and skidded across the floor. Eve pounced on it, scraping her knees in the process. She came up with it and held it on Cecilia, who made no move to get away. The face she raised toward Eve was stained with tears and filled with pain.

"Nice shooting, Cecilia," Eve said.

Cecilia did not hear her. "I waited all these years to be with him, and we were going to be able to live in style for the rest of our lives," she wailed. "And now, it's all over. The dream is over."

"Some dream," Eve said, moving to kick Cecilia's handbag away from her in case it contained more weapons of destruction. Eve was tempted to tell Cecilia she wouldn't need the five million dollars for the hit now because her room and board would be provided for, courtesy of the state and possibly in a tropical paradise. She decided there was no point in rubbing it in.

The couple, who had watched soundlessly and wide eyed through the sequence of events, began moving in an effort to get Eve's attention. "Be with you as soon as I can get a knife to cut you loose."

The woman inclined her head toward a drawer, and Eve opened it without taking her eyes from Cecilia. Fumbling inside with her hand, she came up with a small scout knife she used to cut the woman's ropes. The woman cut her husband loose, and both ran on deck to call for help. In a matter of minutes, the boat was swarming with police and members of the *Clipper*'s crew. Addison was one of the first through the cabin door.

"What the hell!" he exclaimed when he saw Eve, who was covered with new scratches and bruises from her most recent exertions. Her new T-shirt was dirty and torn, and she was still holding the gun on Cecilia. "Are you crazy? Do you think you're John Wayne?"

"I prefer Sheena," she said, handing him the gun.

"Who's Sheena?" he asked.

CHAPTER TWENTY-SIX

They sailed to Saint Vincent the next day and were met by representatives of the FBI and the federal marshal's office. Eve was questioned at the local police station by all concerned and then allowed to return to the ship.

While at the station, however, she did some questioning of her own and learned that Oliver was really Johnny Como, a mob hit man who had just gotten out of prison after serving time on a weapons charge. He was suspected of having killed nine people, but he had never been convicted of anything more serious than manslaughter for one of the alleged hits, the victim having had the bad luck to have stepped in front of Como's speeding car. Como had claimed it was an accident and had served only two years.

"He was very good at what he did, but his luck started to run out when he went to prison on the weapons charge. Now he's dead," Addison said.

"Some people don't learn a thing in prison," Eve quipped. Addison smiled, apparently the only one in the room who appreciated her wit.

"His nickname was 'The Terminator.'"

"How original," Eve remarked.

"Cecilia, Johnny's longtime girlfriend and frequent partner in crime, was really Angelica Marie Reed or Mead or Murphy, whichever name she happened to be using," Addison continued.

"Angelica?" Eve asked.

"Her mother thought so," Addison replied.

"How did they find Tony and Flo?"

"Tapped their kids' phones, as I suspected."

Addison said Angelica had confessed to luring Emory into the lifeboat by pretending she had heard a noise in it. "When he climbed up to investigate, Como, who was hiding under the tarp, shot him. They had decided to get rid of him because Como knew it was only a matter of time before Emory would figure out who he was. The question that no one's been able to answer is how he made Emory so fast and missed me. I guess we'll never know now that Como's dead."

The same question had nagged Eve, and it continued to do so. But for now it remained a mystery.

It turned out the crewman who should have been guarding the gangway when Eve assumed her "Sheena" role had been found in a storage closet, gagged and tied up but unhurt. "And that missing button you noticed on Oliver's—I mean Como's—shirt, it didn't match the one we found in your cabin," Addison said. "You were right about the gun being in Cecilia's bag, but you were wrong about the button. Next time you have a hunch you wish to follow in the middle of the night, take someone with you."

The following day, the *Sun Clipper* sailed for Grenada. Addison remained behind with his colleagues to wrap up loose ends, such as who had jurisdiction. That would take a while. He saw Eve off before the ship left in the morning.

"Here's something to remember your trip by," he said, enjoying his little joke. He shoved a Saint Vincent souvenir T-shirt decorated with a huge purple hibiscus into her hands. Her last *Sun Clipper* T-shirt had been torn in the struggle on the boat. "You really should take better care of your clothes."

"At least I won't have to go home in rags," she said, thanking him.

Their good-byes were more formal than she would have liked because Addison's colleagues were waiting for him.

"I'll call," he said, hugging her lightly.

"Sure," she said, turning away so he couldn't see her tears.

On the trip to Grenada, Harry Goldbaum had already begun collecting the names of passengers for the class-action lawsuit he planned to file against the cruise line when he got back to the States.

"This cruise was an outrage. All our lives were unnecessarily placed at risk. We should have been protected," he told Eve in an indignant voice that probably worked wonders in a courtroom. He was trying to sign her up as one of the representatives of the class.

"You look pretty healthy," Eve said, intentionally eyeing the lawyer's wide girth. "How much do you think our combined outrage is worth?"

"I plan to ask at least thirty million. I think that's fair," he said.

"That's more than the entire cruise line is worth," Eve said.

"That's what insurance is for," he said smugly.

"I hope his plane crashes," Mike said when Eve bumped into him later in the bar. Mike was alone and sipping what appeared to be orange juice. He saw her looking at the glass and waved it in the air. "I'm turning over a new leaf in more ways than one," he said. "I've decided I'm not crazy about the man I've become."

"So who were you with on the beach the other night?" Eve asked.

"I've been seeing one of Kellerman's daughters. Marissa. I think I'm in love with her."

Eve recalled the elegant brown-skinned beauty who had appeared on Kellerman's arm at dinner the night they arrived. She was his youngest daughter from his union with "the island woman."

"Does Kellerman know?"

"I'm not sure. He will if I decide to move to the island and marry her."

She left Mike brooding over his orange juice. She doubted his sudden "change" would be profound or permanent. She only hoped Candy had not been hurt, and she went in search of her to say good-bye.

Candy was in her cabin packing her belongings when Eve knocked. "I wanted to thank you for your help," Eve said.

"Hey, I didn't do much. Oh, I forgot to tell you what I found out about Ridge and Amsterdam, though I guess they're no longer suspects. They're a gay couple who didn't want anyone to know they were traveling together," she said, laughing. "That's why they kept to themselves. Amsterdam's married and probably didn't want his wife to find out."

Eve didn't ask her how she had learned their secret, one that Eve had already guessed after observing them together. The remark Eve had overhead could have been a reference to Amsterdam's intention to end his marriage. As Candy had said, it didn't matter now.

"And you, will you be okay?" Eve asked.

"Yes, I guess the trip was a learning experience for me. I'm going home to try to find out where I stand with my husband. I never told you, but I'm married to a doctor. He's older than I am, and I met him working at the hospital. We've been married five years. No children. Our jobs put a lot of pressure on both of us. A month ago, I found out he was having an affair with his receptionist. I was pretty upset and asked him for a divorce. He wants to work things out, even go to counseling if it will help. He says he still loves me. I don't know how I feel about him. I'm going home to find out."

"And Mike?"

"I was just a fling to him—his usual cruise liaison, I guess. Perhaps my relationship with Mike made me appreciate my husband more. Maybe it evened the score a little. I don't know," Candy said.

"I was married to a man who turned out to have more emotional problems than Carter had liver pills," Eve said. "After a few years, I decided if I wanted to be used as a human punching bag, I could take up boxing and at least get paid. To say the split was not amicable would be an understatement. He missed not having anyone to knock around."

"How did you get through it?"

"I immersed myself in my work and stayed out of his way. I recovered. I guess what I'm trying to say is that one does get through these things. Perhaps your situation isn't so bad."

"Thanks," Candy said, giving Eve a hug. "I'll just see what happens when I get home. You take care."

Eve nodded and noticed that Candy had slipped her wedding ring back on her finger.

Later in the day, Eve ran into Donitsky, who was still carrying his canvas bag. "I can't stand the suspense anymore," Eve said. "You've got to tell me what's in the bag before I go home."

"I already told you, but you didn't believe me. I collect sea shells to make into jewelry," Donitsky said, opening the bag for her. He seemed more relaxed to Eve, as did the other passengers who no longer feared being murdered in their beds.

He withdrew a cellophane package containing a delicate pin made of shells and handed it to her. "It's how I make my living. You keep it," he said. "It's my small way of thanking you for having caught the killer before he killed anyone else."

They had only a half day in Grenada. Eve spent it touring the town and spending time in a picturesque botanical garden specializing in the spices for which the island was known. She picked up souvenirs for her friends.

The next morning, she slipped into the T-shirt Addison had given her and the only pair of shorts that had survived the trip and headed for the airport wondering if she would ever hear from him again. She was standing in line when Mike trotted up to her.

"They found your luggage," he said, a broad grin lighting up his face.

"You're kidding," she said.

He wasn't. An airline official produced the old olive-green Samsonite bag from a pile behind the counter.

"Just take it through customs," the official said, motioning toward a line of travelers some distance away.

"You're kidding," Eve said again. "I've found bodies in my cabin, I've been hit over the head and shot at by someone trying to kill me, and on top of that I haven't had my clothes to wear this whole trip. The suitcase hasn't been out of the airport, and now you expect me to stand in line and go through customs so I can put it back on the plane."

The official blinked once but was unmoved by her tale of woe. "It's our policy," he said, as if that explained everything. She turned to solicit Mike's help, but he was on the other side of the room helping an attractive blond woman she had never seen before lift her luggage onto a conveyor.

"You didn't think he really planned to change," she muttered to no one in particular as she carried her bag to the end of the line.

For an unexplained reason, the flight to Miami was delayed for two hours. By the time it touched down on the runway, the loose end that had bothered Eve ever since Saint Vincent could no longer be ignored. Because of the plane's late arrival, she had missed her connecting flight to Cleveland and had a three-hour layover before catching the next one.

After checking her bag, she took a taxi from the airport and arrived at the *Sun Clipper* office just before closing time. The office was in a low brick building that had a worn look. The staff had left for the day when she sank into a chair across from Albert Sinclair. He was a heavyset man with black hair, bushy eyebrows, and restless eyes.

"So you're Eve—the original woman—the one who cracked the case," he gushed, extending a fleshy hand for her to shake. "Mike told me all about your exploits. Somehow from his description of how you single-handedly took on a killer, I expected to see someone larger. The line owes you a debt of gratitude. You are always welcome to take a cruise free of charge," he said, waving his pudgy hand in the air for emphasis. "I was so glad when you called—"

"I didn't come here for that," Eve said, interrupting him. "I think you know why I'm here, so I'll get right to the point. How much did they pay you to put Como on the cruise and to finger Emory for him?"

Sinclair's eyes flickered, and his face blanched. In that moment, Eve knew she had been right.

"That's ridiculous," Sinclair blustered, recovering himself.

"Hardly," Eve said. "It was you who radioed Como that Emory was arriving. He wrecked the communications room as much to keep us from getting help as to cover the fact that he had gotten a message from you. When the room was destroyed, the call logs were obliterated. You didn't know about Addison because Mike had unwittingly brought him on board as a travel writer. Otherwise he would have been killed too."

"You're crazy. You can't prove any of this," he said.

"I don't think you knew Emory would be killed," Eve continued, ignoring his bluster. "In fact, I'm not sure when you agreed to put Como on your ship that you knew he was a hit man on an assignment. But I am sure it won't be too hard to prove you were paid handsomely for doing it. My guess is that you may have owed the wrong kind of people a few favors. It takes a lot of money to start a cruise-ship line. A look at your books will clear up a lot of questions and provide a clear motive."

Sinclair got up from behind his desk and moved menacingly toward Eve. "You shouldn't have come alone this time," he said quietly. His friendly demeanor was gone, and his dark eyes shone with malice. "I didn't know anyone would be killed, and now I'm an accomplice. You know that I can't let you leave."

Eve got up and backed toward the office door. "I didn't come alone," she said, glad neither she nor Sheena would have to take on another assailant. She had called the FBI office from the airport and talked to one of Emory's former associates. He and two other agents had met her near the *Sun Clipper* office.

As Sinclair began to reach for the gun in his desk drawer, one of the agents who had been listening at the door stepped into the room and leveled his gun at him. "Keep your hands where I can see them. You have the right to remain silent..." he began, after the second agent had frisked and handcuffed Sinclair.

Eve left the room and used an office phone to call a taxi for her ride back to the airport. The rest of the trip to Cleveland was uneventful.

When she arrived, the same tired gray snow lay in piles along the highway as she drove from the airport toward downtown. A light drizzle had begun, melting what lay at the edge of the road and turning it into a sea of dingy slush. So much had happened to her in the past week, but so little had changed here, she thought, suddenly realizing how much she had missed the grit of the city.

When she opened her apartment door, Keats hurled himself through the air and landed on her right eyebrow, where he clung precariously until she lifted him to her shoulder. He was glad to see her. Eve was happy to see he hadn't become stressed out and lost all of his feathers or died from eating Irene's rich food.

She avoided Irene. She dreaded the inevitable meeting when she would have to admit that Irene's predictions of danger and death on the cruise had been true. Of course, technically Irene had been wrong about Eve's being the intended victim. However, Irene would consider that a minor detail, especially when Eve confessed to being nearly drowned in a leaky boat, run over by a freighter, knocked senseless by a killer, and shot at and threatened with annihilation by Sinclair. The events of the cruise and its aftermath would, no doubt, strengthen Irene's belief in her premonitions, and Eve hated to encourage her.

Bright and early Monday morning, Eve showed up at the office for work. She was exhausted from her ordeal. Her body ached from numerous scrapes and bruises, which she had tried to cover either with makeup or clothing. Her head still hurt when she moved too quickly. With luck, she planned to spend her first day back in a sedentary position catching up on phone messages and mail. She might even contemplate ways to salvage a travel story out of the cruise from hell, but she doubted even her writing skills were up to the task. Besides, she had to acknowledge that she may have personally sunk the *Sun Clipper* line for good. It seemed unlikely that it could recover with Sinclair no longer available to run it. The beautiful yacht and the others owned by the line would most likely have to be sold to pay his debts and for his legal defense.

Perhaps she could write a first-person account of the events in the Caribbean, which had not made the papers in Cleveland, thus giving the *Tribune* a coveted local angle. The newspaper's editors decided years ago that if it didn't happen in the city, a nearby suburb, or have a strong local connection, it wasn't news their readers would be interested in.

"So how was the trip?" Wally asked without looking up from his computer terminal. Eve wondered if he had moved since she last saw him.

"I've had better," Eve said, considering whether to elaborate.

"I hope you're rested," Wally said, ignoring her quasi-complaint. "I've got a triple homicide I want you to work on. It happened near W. 46th. Could have been a hit. You know, organized crime. The police aren't saying. You need to get ahold of your sources."

"You're kidding," Eve said.

He shook his head. "In case you forgot, while you were flitting around the Caribbean and basking in the sun, we have deadlines and a newspaper to run. You'd better get moving. Vacation's over."

At least that was something to be thankful for, Eve thought, picking up her notebook and shrugging on her coat.

Made in the USA
Lexington, KY
28 July 2018